ACTS OF TRUST

A MEDITATION UPON LOVE

James R Warren

BLOXWICH
2025

Published in the United Kingdom in 2025 by
Midland Tutorial Productions

First Edition: 1 October 2025

File Prefix Code: AOT

ISBN 978 1 915750 14 3

Email: MTP1586@gmail.com

ACTS OF TRUST
A MEDITATION UPON LOVE

James R Warren

MIDLAND TUTORIAL PRODUCTIONS
BLOXWICH

Other Books By James R Warren

Boscawen-Ûn
Beyond Tourist Britain
Gleanings as I Pass
Exordium
Meditations
Gamma Solution
Moddeshall Hydropower
Unreasonable Mathematics
Mathematical Explorations
Researches: Volume One
Researches: Volume Two
Researches: Volume Three
Researches: Volume Four
Pi and Phi
Four Famous Numbers
Progress in Iron Smelting
Congleholme

AUTHORIAL STATEMENT

"Acts of Trust" discusses controversial psychosexual
procreative and Sacramental practices,
which some might find unacceptable in
religious or existential discourse.

I do not advocate non-consensual corporal punishment.
Corporal punishment is torture and torture is evil.

Consensual beatings, for those able to consent,
whether as sex play or religious penance,
are ethical but like all bodily procedures
are hazardous and must be managed
with extreme care.

PLEASE DO NOT GIFT THIS BOOK TO A CHILD OR TO ANYONE WHO MAY BE DISTURBED OR OFFENDED BY THE TEXT

All scenes are fictional.

Names were created intentionally to be unusual but credible.
The identity or similarity of names to living persons is
fortuitous.

Thank you for your purchase.
Enjoy your read and whatever your beliefs
take your time to think or to pray.
May God Bless You.

JR Warren

AOT
WARREN

FOR

Those Who Dare to Love

AOT
WARREN

TABLE OF CONTENTS

Cheap grace means grace sold on the market like cheapjack's wares. The sacraments, the forgiveness of sin and the consolations of religion are thrown away at cut prices. Grace is represented as the Church's inexhaustible treasury, from which she showers blessings with generous hands, without asking questions or fixing limits. Grace without price, grace without cost! The essence of grace we suppose, is that the account has been paid in advance; and, because it has been paid, everything can be had for nothing. Since the cost was infinite, the possibilities of using and spending it are infinite. What would grace be if it were not cheap?

Cheap grace means grace as a doctrine, a principle, a system. It means forgiveness of sins proclaimed as a general truth, the love of God taught as the Christian 'conception' of God. An intellectual assent to that idea is held to be of itself sufficient to secure remission of sins. The Church which holds the correct doctrine of grace has, it is supposed, *ipso facto* a part in that grace. In such a Church the world finds a cheap covering for its sins; no contrition is required, still less any real desire to be delivered from sin. Cheap grace therefore amounts to a denial of the living Word of God, in fact, a denial of the Incarnation of the Word of God.

Cheap grace means the justification of sin without the justification of the sinner.

-Dietrich Bonhoeffer
Nachfolge (The Cost of Discipleship)
Munich, 1937AD
Translated from the German by
RH Fuller and Irmgard Booth

Bonhoeffer was a hard man. But life is hard and death harder. For sure Discipleship is costly, and of course Bonhoeffer's took him to the gallows.

The present author is a less intelligent man than Bonhoeffer was and a much worse person. But I am soft, and seek goodness with only moderate pain and even less inconvenience.

So that is what Grace is then: The forgiveness of sins. I have spent seventy of my seventy-three years wondering. Bonhoeffer's worldview is very German. He sees no irony or oxymoron in phrases like 'general truth' or 'correct doctrine'. In Bonhoeffer's world there is Evil, but no Free Will: Heresy but no doubt.

I call myself a Quaker. But I am a very bad man and an even worse Quaker. I am at least a Christian in the technical sense that I believe that Jesus Christ rose from the dead. For my part, I am almost as convinced of the reality of Free Will as I am of the Resurrection, though I reject doctrine and despise ideology. I believe that Works count in our favor, and I suppose that doctrinally I am more Catholic than Protestant, but I do not really know, and have little inclination to find out. For my part, simple faith and a childlike acceptance of the Words of Christ are necessary and sufficient. Yes, my words are paradoxical, but life is paradox.

Courage and Humility are the father and mother of all virtues.

I suppose the Ancients would have agreed for courage but scorned humility. Would you trust a prideful coward?

What is Trust?

What is Grace?

What is Action?

We may be heretics. We are certainly explorers. For the only certainty is that we are uncertain. An uncertain person has to be humble, and an explorer brave. In paraphrase of Chesterton we possess an "awful liberty of [our] lonely souls" and it is that liberty and that solitude which is God's Gift to Man: Man's choice at Man's risk.

Love is no mere affect. Love is an election, leading to action, an Act of Trust. A marriage is an Act of Trust. A confession is an Act of Trust. So is any sacrifice. So is a declaration of war.

AOT
WARREN

CHAPTER ONE
PRINCIPLES

Both the Existence of God and the non-existence of god are logically impossible. But the former is, on balance, the more probable, and certainly the more congenial.

The Life that God begat is very unlikely indeed, but apparently here.

If that life is not an involuntary emanation of His Thought then even larger and more disturbing questions arise.

And if the genesis of matter was virtually instantaneous then the implication is that its annihilation is also a summary event.

Notwithstanding my indefinite discursion you can safely take it from me that God exists, that we are continuing to frustrate His best efforts, and that He is keeping His eye on us.

Life is a campaign activity. Its costs are often exorbitant and ultimately total. We should respect the life we have been lent, as we cherish the lives of the creatures about us.

To despise life is an insult to God and a repudiation of His ideas. To despise life is cruelty and cruelty brings sin. Christians believe that our sins are forever reprieved of our recompense in Hell by the final and sufficient Sacrifice of Our Holy Savior. Notwithstanding this, you suffer in this life the guilt, hate and alienation your cruelties bring. You strive to forgive yourself and for the forgiveness of those you value, and you look to a better future.

I am almost certainly more evil than you. I too seek forgiveness of God and man. I should pray for your forgiveness and your spiritual refreshment. I should hope you pray for mine.

The human mind coheres aspects of the animal and the Divine. The problem is that God is not an animal, at least not in any sense comprehensible to a human or his collective. There is an existential mis-match.

Part of the problem is simply that His thoughts are not our thoughts. (This is not my idea: It says so in The Bible). This is not a failing of God, neither a spite of any agent. The difficulty resides with human beings. It arises from natural limitations upon the intellectual power that we can focus on problems.

To refuse the image for the word is a fatal error, for to prefer the symbol to the res represented is the antithesis of reason. The fathers put aside the naked and the nude, and soothing scenes of tranquil pastures, as supposed idolatry. Minds focused upon the text rather than its Meaning, a sign of madness. The image of the real was clothed in the vacancy of limewash, or, even more disastrously, with geometrical patterning, as if to raise the genius of Euclid higher than the immanence of God.

To refuse the reality for the image is a fatal error, for to prefer the likeness to the res represented is the antithesis of nature. The Moderns put aside the painful and insanitary immediacies of experience and focused upon the picture and its schema rather than its object, a sign of evasion. The image of the real was invested with a film of glossy abstraction, or, even more disastrously, a specious aura of definitive veracity, as if to raise the idealisations of Leonardo above the fabric of Creation.

The virtues of the European Enlightenment: Trust, Humaneness, Naturalism, and Reason brought us very far but can go little further without supplement. Reason is a luxury of the leisured. Human beings quite simply are not rational, for if they were they would never have evolved, and would hardly have been made irrational by a Creator. If they were rational they certainly would not do anything inimical to individual or collective survival. By the first half of the Nineteenth Century it was already clear to advanced thinkers, both in mathematics and philosophy, that people needed something extra.

I believe that there is some sense of meaning in which God made the world, and living things are a spawn of his consciousness. But His historical behaviour shows that our condition grieves him and that he is ready to attempt improvements where he can, and in particular where we let him. If God really were Almighty then Paradise would be ubiquitous. I am not saying we control God. That would be absurd. I am saying there is such a thing as Free Will. We can freely choose good or evil, for ourselves and for those under our power.

The human species (and all kinds of animal) has a range of social behaviours adapted to reproduction and other survival imperatives. In principle, any of these tendencies can be exploited to make men and women more God-like, and thus bridge part of the chasm between God and Man. Any attempt to approach God is highly dangerous but the rewards of success, or even partial success, are indescribably grand.

The Doctrine of Agency

The Doctrine of Agency is the essential philosophical basis of the Christian faith. Theological theory views Christ both as the intercessor between God and Man, and also as God in Person. Therefore there is some sense in which Christ is an Agent of God's Will, or, if you will excuse my vulgar language, the middleman who brokers the commerce of God and Man.

Pastors and priests are also agents, including such as Quakers and Rosicrucians who assist one another on a basis of equality under God.

A Confessor is an agent who assists and expedites the congress of a Penitent with God.

<u>The Doctrine of Complementarity</u>

The Doctrine of Complementarity concerns the activities of two inherently-associated dynamics which interact with each other in order to propagate a third entity through time or space.

For example, magnetism and electricity interact to progress the movement of light through space. Without either magnetism or electricity there would be no such thing as light, or any sort of electromagnetic radiation. Potential and kinetic energies share an analogous role in dynamics, and chemical and electrical energy in storage cells. Indeed, such complementarities are ubiquitous throughout science and engineering.

It is an essential property of propagative complementarities that they are equal and reciprocal. It is also characteristic that they play off one another.

Male and Female are complements. Without both a developed biological species, for example *Homo sapiens*, could not propagate through time. Male and Female are equal and opposite. It is in some respects arbitrary to claim that the male is active and dominant and the female passive and submissive: They are essentially in a state of dynamic counterpoise and neither could act without the other. An animal in possession of a Y-chromosome is technically male even if its anatomy and behavior are very feminine but we must be careful in difficult cases to distinguish between the essential and the accidental.

By way of further example, and if we narrow the focus to the rôles of male and female in fecund partnership, we can adjudge that the Protection of the Male is complementary to the Obedience of the Female. It is impossible to protect a mobile and intellectual partner who will not co-operate; it is impossible to propagate from a partner who neither survives nor co-operates; and it is impossible for humans to propagate asexually.

The failure of one or both of the propagative complements results in extinction of the dependant third principal, and in the case of a biological species this is tantamount to the extinction of the species itself.

Similarly, one may naturally think that a Confessor is dominant and his or her Penitent submissive. But neither can act without the other. They are equal and complementary. To speak metaphorically, both sit at the Feet of God. The Confessor and the Penitent collaborate to make the other more of a person that God wants them to be, and by so doing they augment the happiness of a wider collective, and increase the probability of its survival.

The Limits of Language

I have taken to saying this so often in my works that it has long been tiresome. And for that I apologise. Nevertheless, I shall say it again.

The English language evolved to solve the routine problems of sailors and shepherds, and of course other skilled people who needed short but effective exchanges of instruction.

Even today language is ill-fitted to the discussion of ethological or psychological issues, let alone the theological or the ontological. Even a man of my education struggles to say what he wants to say, and is inevitably never satisfied by the way he puts things. I hardly need to remind any adult reading this that such things as love or spanking are wholly existential and useful description is impossible. Only personal experience of these effects is informative.

For example, what on God's good earth is a "transverberation"? When we see a picture representing the Transverberation of Theresa we instinctively perceive what manner of thing is being illustrated, but we would be at a loss to describe it in words, and think we know for fact that we ourselves shall never bear such a shock, nor so holy and entire a pleasure, nor ever be able to.

<u>Good and Evil</u>

I believe in the historicity of Jesus Christ and that he was the Agent of God. God is indescribable, intellectual and permeative. We cannot *define* the Works of God. For sure, we may partially *describe* aspects of His works, for example, electromagnetic radiation or fluid flow. But our descriptions always depend upon the use of codes and languages all of which are works of men and accordingly are only metaphorical. When I tell you that a field influence diminishes as an inverse square I am inviting you to fit a geometrical abstraction to a natural decline: There is an existential mis-match. Geometry is a metaphor. Of course, we can also cite quantum entanglement or morphic resonance or something else as explanations of physical manifestations, but all these too are metaphors.

I shall not invite you to believe in the personality of Satan. Rather Satan is a metaphor for an intellectual and permeative presence rather (and this is another metaphor) like the apparently unthinking force of gravity. We are told that gravity is a warp in the space-time continuum that impels matter to some inevitable if very distant singularity at which the matter enters an altered but unknowable state. We are also told that it is the matter itself that somehow engenders the warp. Similarly, Evil is a warp in the fabric of spiritual relationships that distorts the Soul and impels men and women to the destruction of the self and of each other. Paradoxically, Evil is ubiquitous and permeative, but can be defied. Just as Good can, unfortunately, be defied.

As men and women we should do something very difficult, perhaps impossible without God's Help. We should transform hate into love, pain into pleasure, intolerance into acceptance, and the omnipresence of death into vibrant life, now and for ever. For certain, this cannot destroy Evil: What animal can perturb a metaphysical force? But such transformations can bring us solace at the Feet of God, now and for ever.

Violence
====

The very great danger with violence is its casualisation and habituation to a routine or formalism. We readily apprehend, at the level of microcosm, that the danger of habituation afflicts some of the Christian Domestic Discipline and Loving Domestic Discipline couples discussed elsewhere in this disquisition. It also affects, or perhaps I should say infects, American gun culture and worldwide militarism. Violence is special. Violence is the recourse when reasoning, persuasion, bribery and even begging have failed. Violence should be the last resort.

I hate violence, and have since being a very small boy indeed.

Violence is evil.

But total abstinence from all violence can allow other evils to prosper rankly.

Spanking is violence.

Spanking is also of its nature limited in its *physical* destructive effect if somewhat absurd. But like any violence, spanking, when rarely applied as a special and privileged event can arrest or prevent other, sometimes more serious, evils.

The evils arrested can even include, or indeed wholly comprise, evils that damage the perpetrator.

A feature of corporal acts, and especially spanking, is that they can be interpreted as humiliations or even sexual assaults, especially by male subjects. For this reason, any sacramental use of spanking has to be approached with extreme tact and humility, especially by whoever is handing-down the spanks.

In Britain and America, spanking, however defined, has a very evil history. Christianity is about Redemption through Suffering in Imitation of Christ. The essence of Christian piety is the transformation of Evil to Good.

CHAPTER TWO
LOVE AS WONDER

<u>First Thoughts</u>

Love is the least rational of emotions. But we would be lost without it. For many years I loved disused lead mines. For love is the natural patrimony of lost and lonely things. But what is this thing we call "loss"? In all of literature it seems that Love and Loss conjugate ineluctably, even naturally, like bread and butter, like bread and wine.

It is the nature of Love to lose and be lost, and yet the loss of love is never like losing a credit card. The loss of a credit card is somehow frantic and urgent, a race against the interloper and the opportunist. The loss of love is somehow stately and slowly sad, grieving and resigned, always mournful, ever mourned, though the love itself is never regretted.

The natural province of love and loss is the howling waste, the high forgotten moors of England, the deserts of the Levant or the ice-girt Polar seas.

For though ardent deserts scorch the last long fate of love is the frozen fastness of rest, like the final pit of Perdition, or the universal Heat Death of Victorian thermodynamics, for love is hopeless, unless Love persists in Paradise.

It is the nature of Love to conjugate, to attract, as might Man and Woman, opposing poles, or some other accidents of affinity.

For the love of self is infecund, and dies the death.

We need not consult the objective merit, if any, of the object loved. It is notorious that the most unlovely things are often the best loved, and most loyally, for the love of evil abounds, and is very well-documented. Barabbas was loved. So was Hitler. So is Satan.

Jesus Crist loves the unloved, the leper, the lunatic, the rejected and abandoned. Christ loves without hate, without cruelty.

You love your country and you are entitled to do so, and you rightly enjoy your love and your sacrifice. But unless you are a mindless bigot you are well aware of its cruelties and its defects, both historical and present, and of the needs of others to offer and receive Love, however they frame it.

We may speak of what Love may be, and yet never define it, for all the finest features of existence are indelineable. To analyse the beloved, as might a critic or a savant, is to assess and maybe to like or approve, rather than to love.

Like all judgment, assessment and analysis is finite in its incompleteness, and yet Love is infinite and entire.

Love does not seek approval or reciprocation. Love is self-absorbed in the apprehension of its object: Accepting, forbearing, tender and contemplative.

Love is not Friendship.

Whatever they may tell themselves, or each other, lovers seldom have much in common. Love is possible between black and white, thick and thin, or as Blake might have put it, "Heathen, Turk and Jew." (William Blake, "The Divine Image", Stanza 5).

Love does not ask: "Is this beauty?"

Love does not ask: "Is this truth?"

Love nor Beauty nor Truth are Information, as others have observed.

We were told to love our enemies. And such an outrage is indeed possible, because to love is not necessarily to agree, approve or ally. To love is to excuse, to tolerate, to create, to make space for, as space is created *ex nihilo* for an expanding universe, or a lost tribe homing.

Christ Himself spent forty days and forty nights in the hungry desert learning to love, and to love the right thing. Loving the right is the best decision a man can make, and for men it is the most fraught and difficult of mental applications.

Love is not easy.

Second Thoughts

You may object that Satan is a metaphor. But what a metaphor! The greatest art describes his doings. For the Metaphor mirrors the minds of men. John Milton was a seventeenth-century English poet who explored the nature of Good and Evil and Satan's rejection of God in an epic poem "*Paradise Lost*". I cannot improve the overview of Satan's attitudes to Love as offered by Generative AI, let alone John Milton, and accordingly I take the liberty of quoting the computer utility verbatim:-

> "In classical literature, Satan, often a figure of rebellion and self-absorbed power, views love as a weakness and a tool for manipulation and destruction, rather than a source of connection or virtue.
>
> Here's a more detailed look at Satan's perspective on love in classical literature, particularly as depicted in Milton's Paradise Lost:
>
> ***Love as a Tool for Rebellion***:
>
> Satan's primary motivation is to overthrow God and establish his own dominion, and he views love as a weakness that can be exploited to achieve his goals.
>
> ***Self-Love and Pride***:
>
> Satan's love for himself and his own power becomes a central theme, leading him to reject any form of humility or submission to a higher authority.

Distortion of Love:
Satan manipulates the concept of love to suit his purposes, often twisting it into a form of lust or self-gratification rather than a genuine connection.
Satan as a Fallen Hero:
Some interpretations of Paradise Lost suggest that Satan is portrayed as a complex and even sympathetic figure, with his actions stemming from a sense of injustice and a desire for freedom, even if misguided.
Example in Paradise Lost:
In Book 9, Satan uses flattery and manipulation to tempt Eve, exploiting her desire for knowledge and independence, rather than genuine love or affection.
Contrast with Christian Virtue:
Milton contrasts Satan's flawed view of love with the Christian ideals of love, mercy, and humility, which are exemplified by God and Christ."

So Satan is really the epitome and archetype of human Evil, encapsulating the perverse perfections of Pride, Cruelty, Selfishness, Grievance and Entitlement. But Satan inheres another tendency only rarely found in the human Spirit: A determinate will to invert virtue, to pervert Love against itself, and to mock God.

If we are misguided then we must be careful that we are not actually being guided from outwith: Being manipulated by Satan. The old poet-prophets of the Abrahamic tradition alleged that Satan existed before Man and that his original grievance was that God begat a Son and favored that Son.

Jealousy is the most malign of spiteful vices, and the least manly or womanly. Be sedulous to resist it. I seldom managed, to my eternal dishonor.

But enough of Evil for the meantime.

This book is about pleasant, Sacramental things like Love, Marriage, Confession, Penance and Reformation.

What could be lovelier than kneeling with your deeply Beloved and reading together the divine sutras of her Faith, or praying to our common God?

Ideology is an artifice, and breeding an adaption for the propagation of species, so the race or religion of your wife or husband is a mere detail, irrelevant to your shared love of tolerance, mercy and the cheerful acceptance of one another as Images of God.

Perhaps the Ancient concept of "Image" (εἰκών) is slightly unfortunate in the Modern mind, connoting as it does a literal physical appearance. The Ancients thought more, as we would say, in terms of "likeness", in the sense that men and women are "similar to" God, partaking as Shakespeare said, of several God-like powers and appointments, though not true Knowledge, nor everlasting Life.

Third Thoughts

If you mean to defeat Satan, arm yourself, as you are entitled to do in defence of your kin and country. But take especial care of your most potent weapons: Love, Mercy and Humility, as even computers recommend for us.

Being humble and submissive is not about being a sap or a coward or a doormat.

Being humble and submissive is about being an animal conscious of his transience and his frailty as an Image of God, not its Substance.

Being humble and submissive is about being clever enough to appreciate that you do not know all the answers, and neither shall you learn enough in this life.

Being humble and submissive is about being brave, and cheerfully walking in the Way.

Being humble and submissive is not about adopting grievance, or prosecuting the grievances of others, in order to magnify yourself.

Being humble and submissive is about the practice of any valid Faith, that is a faith that enjoins humility, obedience and compassion.

As has often been pointed out, including by Christ Himself, loving our friends is easy. As Christ also made clear we should also love our enemies and those who have spited us. That is difficult.

It is very difficult indeed to put aside anger, respect the transgressor, and correct him firmly but humanely, without pride, sanctimony, vengefulness, self-gratification or other wickedness, in a way which builds, makes *the enemy's* life better, and keeps the peace.

For example, the thorny problem of what to do with wretches like murderers, rapists and other torturers, or pedophiles? For my part, I wonder what useful purpose is served *to anyone* by handing-down the Whole Life Sentence or even "life" sentences in excess of (say) ten years. I have been an opponent of capital punishment since boyhood, but I have sometimes asked myself if people sentenced to more than ten years' incarceration should not be offered, with their consent, death. After all, and unforgivably, that is what we now offer to the disabled and the desperate, with their ostensible consent.

Criminals should be firmly punished for sure, but should they also be trained to reform morally and lead harmless and useful lives, or is that an abuse of will?

Clearly, some criminal tendencies such as sexual perversions are the result of mental illness, and the ethics of punishing the mad is problematical, just as their treatment may be an abuse of the body and mind.

I do not pretend to know The Answer. All must avoid judgment and condemnation, but co-operate in preserving the peace and the welfare of the individual, in so far as he accepts help.

It is much better to apply the gentler corrective, as long as it solves the problem, rather than a brutal or protracted solution such as killing or divorce.

So penalties should be firm and condign, but building and respectful, informed by Love not retribution.

Not all of us have the ability to share in Life, Liberty and the Pursuit of Happiness, but all of us have the Liberty to Love.

Fourth Thoughts

The dermapteran beetle called the European Earwig (*Forficula auricularia*) is extremely common in the UK. As an adult it is around fifteen millimeters in length, with a flattened, slender profile. It is instantly recognised by the cerci or "pincers" that it sports from its rear.

It is a shy, inoffensive, yet much loathed, creature who prefers to shelter with its kind in damp cervices under rocks or in rotten wood during the daylight hours.

It is mostly saprophagous (feeding on dead matter) but will sometimes attack small fauna or living vegetation opportunistically, earning the obloquy of gardeners.

The rear cerci are rich in nerve endings and earwigs use them during sexual activity as well as as weapons, which can award humans a nasty pinch!

Less than one percent of any insects care for their young but earwigs, especially the females, are most diligent parents.

The photograph shown below was taken at Chester, England in 2020, when a house brick was lifted from the ground to expose a mother with her numerous hatched and unhatched offspring.

Photo: Tom Oatcs, 2020

**A Female European Earwig
Tends Her Brood**

The female who guards the nest is not necessarily the mother of all the eggs or nymphs. She is able to distinguish other females' eggs in her nest by their smell, but will tend them just as assiduously as her own. Her care includes the regular striping of parasitic fungus which forms on the eggs, as well as fortifying the young by coating them with hydrocarbons in the same way that a gardener might coat a wooden shed with creosote, to deter earwigs and others.

Is this altruism?

If a spider or scorpion attempts to poach the eggs or the wiglets the female will use her scissor-like cerci to dismember and disarm it, and then doubtless eat and regurgitate the predator's tissue to feed her wiglets, for their diet is a constant supply of regurgitated pap from the mother. If there is a grass fire, the female will rescue the young one-by-one to a place of safety, even at the cost of her own life.

Is this love? Is this courage?

You may reply that she is merely manifesting animal instinct as an automaton.

But is that what men and women do? Manifest animal instinct, like any good parents, or those who give thought for their community?

Should we love the earwigs, and if so what is the best way of expressing our love for them?

AOT
WARREN

CHAPTER THREE
LOVE AS SIN

The test of virtue is Conducement. Does the virtue conduce to a beneficent outcome? Does the virtue conduce to the procreation of the species? Does it ameliorate the bad? Does it increase the happiness of the individual?

Love is a virtue.

Is the love selfish?

Virtue can congeal to vice.

Sin is any cruelty that you inflict. It is not necessarily malicious or consciously intended. Sin always has a living victim, and it hurts or harms your victim. God qualifies as a living victim. So, potentially, do you.

You are not born sinful: Only with the capacity to sin.

In this discussion of sin I shall say little of evil people who act with malice, or people who commit serious statute crimes. They need pastoral support for sure, and some would benefit from confessional penance. But they have complex needs and require the care of medical and penal specialists.

You are a good person and your needs differ.

Over and above human conceptions of sin are the imperative Commandments of God that were handed down to Moses as he wondered through the desert. They are listed in Chapter Twenty of Exodus and again in Deuteronomy 5:1-21. Adapting the Commandments of God for the rich young man (Matthew 19:16-22) Our Holy Savior said: "Do not kill", "Do not steal", "Do not commit adultery", "Do not bear false witness", "Love thy neighbor", and "Honor your Father and Mother".

Using modern language these Ten Commandments of God are in order:-

1	Have No Other Gods
2	Make No Idols
3	Do Not Take God's Name in Vain
4	Keep the Sabbath Holy
5	Honor Your Father and Mother
6	Do Not Kill
7	Do Not Commit Adultery
8	Do Not Steal
9	Do Not Lie to Get Someone into Trouble
10	Do Not Be Jealous

If these articles are obeyed men live like angels. To our lasting cost many disobey each by habit and all break some on occasion.

To disobey the Injunctions of Christ or any Commandment of God is a Mortal Sin. It is a very serious matter that is always hurtful. You have noticed something else about Mortal Sins: They usually involve concealment or some other act of cowardice.

In an attempt to be helpful, Pope Gregory the First compiled a list of Seven Deadly Sins which are also confessable. He followed specifications in The Bible.

Here is a list of Pope Gregory's sins or vices with their corresponding virtues:-

Sin	*Virtue*
Lust	Chastity
Gluttony	Temperance
Greed	Charity
Sloth	Diligence

Wrath	Patience
Envy	Kindness
Pride	Humility

Gregory's list is only a guide. You will know if you have sinned, and if you need a technical diagnosis a little meditation may yield it. Gregory's sins tend to divide into sins of the mind (Pride, Envy and Wrath) and sins of the flesh (Sloth, Greed, Gluttony and Lust). But of course these evils overlap and interpenetrate. A problem with the Deadly Sins is that they are not actions but thoughts that promote action, and thoughts are not sinful of themselves. On the other hand they are a useful list of tendencies to be suppressed.

Sins are formulated in your mind, or arise from a culpable absence of care. Carelessness and indolence are sins of Sloth. You cannot blame Satan or anyone else for your own shortcomings. Satan, too, is a helpless bystander, utterly reliant upon your exercise of Free Will.

It is possible to sin against God though the normal layman can only do so in the one way. God's Third Commandment says you should not take His name in vain. This means you do not call his name unless you truly want him to listen and to help you become the person He wants you to be, or to help some creature you find it hard to help yourself. You do not call him as a matter of ceremony, to progress some kind of administrative procedure, or to impress your friends. You certainly do not do so by stupid habit. Swearing on the Bible in a court of law is blasphemy. The court is the court of your king, not of God. Render unto God the things that are of God, and unto Caesar the things that are Caesar's (Matthew 22:21).

If you call out the Name of God without expecting him to respond you are as much a coward as if you unwarrantably called out for your king or president, whilst being safely out of earshot. Real men and real women do not swear.

The antithesis of swearing is prayer. When you pray you sincerely want God to hear and to act. You are ready to face him. You know that if you abuse the call you could be punished most grievously, unless He is merciful, though He has proven himself to be so. Prayer is for real men and women.

When I was an atheist swearing had no effect on me. Probably I did not notice most of it. If I swore I thought nothing of it. When I swear now, and I just did, I know I am a disgusting coward and hypocrite. Every time I hear the words it is like a whiplash upon my soul.

Blasphemy defiles a man, as prayer sounds sweet upon the lips of a woman and a curse of complaint unfruitful.

Minced oaths are just extra craven ones, as they imply that whilst we have dismissed the appearance of God as too improbable to fear, yet we live in terror of the censure of men. These include the British swearword "bloody", the one that crossed my lips, and the vocative expression "for fuck's sake", that traduces not only the Divine itself but also a sacred act appointed of it.

A man or woman is before me and he or she blasphemes on feeling sudden acute pain. Do not think that I do not understand. Do not think that I am unsympathetic. My heart is with them. Whatever happens next, they are a much better person than I.

Please do not swear.

It is possible to sin against yourself, but whilst the sin may cause you pain, it is your loved ones who suffer. Lust, Gluttony and Sloth are sins against the self. Who pays when you indulge yourself? Think about it.

Pride is the source of many of the sins and real crimes committed by men and women who try to do good.

In 2008 my new neighbor moved in. His new house had been unoccupied for nearly a year and a summer's growth luxuriated his garden and the Leylandii hedge that bounded it. Proudly and industriously he trimmed these high untidy hedges and he made a very good job of so doing. He and his were very happy to enter their new home. I wonder if he spared a thought for the tiny creatures who lost theirs. Disconsolate little birds spent the day fluttering through my shrubbery, distressing themselves and their neighbors. Would you like your home destroyed? Pride had led to cruelty.

A few days later I passed an angler beside a canal. He was torturing small fish. He was about forty years old and if you are foreign you possibly wonder that a grown man would, but I digress. He accosted me to ask that I take pictures of him and then revealed a magnificent dying pike from a keep net. I asked him if he was going to eat it but he said he would place it back in the canal. He posed with the fish but was dissatisfied with my captures. Cruelty had led to Pride and then to Wrath.

The gentle snails *Helix Aspersa* love my garden (or is it their garden?), and when it rains come out to graze. When I open gates or pace the tarmac I often forget to look out for them. Proudly I prefer my thoughts. I crush the life from them, violating the Sixth Commandment of God. This is a Mortal Sin arising from Pride and nothing less avuncular than my Deadly Sin of Sloth.

Real men do not kill. Real men pass their Sacred Seed of Life to a woman. Real women bear the new life of which they were Entrusted, and nurture it.

Please do not kill.

<u>Tribe and Party</u>

Almost everyone named in the following narrative was a Christian man or woman who attended Confession regularly according to his rite. Most of them were highly principled. There is one exception. And that exception was a man of the highest judgment and probity.

One day, not so long ago, but in a fairytale country, thirty-year-old Rudolf and his seventeen-year-old mistress Marie were having dinner in their remote hunting lodge. Rudolf's father told him to leave Marie, but Rudolf broke the Fifth Commandment. It was a bleak and snowy January night outside. The furniture was spartan but the food lavish and Rudolf ordered another bottle of his favorite champagne. Perhaps it is harsh to judge young Marie, but Rudolf had also broken the Seventh Commandment, and knew it. Very surprisingly, for the roads were almost snowbound, a deputation arrived. No one knows what happened next but when Rudolf and his lover were found their corpses betrayed signs of extreme violence and at least Rudolf had taken a bullet. Someone had suffered Wrath and broken the Sixth Commandment.

Rudolf's inheritance passed to his fifty-six year old uncle Karl who quickly demurred and passed the poisoned chalice to his twenty-five-year old son, Franz Ferdinand.

Ten years passed.

Franz Ferdinand went to see his aging uncle, Franz Josef. Franz Ferdinand, now in his late thirties, had some very good news. He had proposed marriage to the love of his life, Sophie, and she had accepted. Franz Ferdinand asked his uncle Franz Josef for permission to marry, for although he was of age, custom demanded such.

Franz Josef filled with wrath. He told his nephew that permission was refused on the grounds that Sophie was a Czech and a mere aristocrat. Racism and snobbery are evils borne of Pride, and have very strange and unlooked-for results, as we shall discover. Franz Josef had forgotten that his sacred duty to love his country and his class must not be adulterated with hate for any. Secondly, Franz Josef told Franz Ferdinand that if he married Sophie he and his heirs would be disinherited. Thirdly, and perhaps most cruelly, Franz Josef specified that henceforth Franz Ferdinand and Sophie should never be seen together in public, except on military business.

Franz Ferdinand exercised his human right freely to choose and marry his life partner, and beget her children. Franz Ferdinand and Sophie wed.

On 28th June 1900, Franz Ferdinand swore a morganatic oath that deprived he and his heirs of the throne of Austria forever. Franz Ferdinand broke the Third Commandment. He also disobeyed Christ's Injunction about hair color. (Matthew 5:36).

Franz Ferdinand decided to spend the fourteenth anniversary of his oath inspecting his uncle's army in Bosnia. He appeared to regard the day as a kind of commemoration, perhaps of his liberation to married bliss and fatherhood. It meant he could be far from Vienna and with his beloved, out and around the sunlit streets of Sarajevo. Old photographs show the couple beaming nervously but delightedly to well-wishers and shaking hands, she with her bouquet of red roses, he in his army uniform.

June 28th, St Vitus Day, dawned hot and dusty. On that day five hundred and twenty-five years previously a Serb had killed the Sultan of Turkey. It was a national holiday. Gavrilo loved his country and his woman above life itself. Gavrilo was nineteen. Gavrilo slipped his FN1910 9mm semi-automatic into his pocket. He went out to meet his friends.

Franz Ferdinand and Sophie went to Mass. They took the brief train ride to the Bosnian capital and alighted. They climbed into their green Gräf und Stift Rois de Blougnie open tourer to be driven about their duties.

The Appel Quay is a leafy lungotevere beside the River Miljacka. At ten that morning, the couple left the barracks and drove along the Appel Quay to the Town Hall, where Franz Ferdinand would recite his prepared speech. In the garden of the Mostar Cafe Mehmed waited to kill them. He chickened-out. Further on, Vaso, too, had a bomb and a gun. He too chickened-out.

At 1010 the royal car approached Nedeljko. He threw a grenade. The driver put his foot down, and the bomb bounced from Franz Ferdinand's car, and did not explode until a following aides' car was above it. Twenty were injured. Nedeljko chewed his cyanide pill, but it failed to kill him. So he jumped into the Miljacka which proved to be four inches deep. He was arrested. Franz Ferdinand and Sophie continued to the Town Hall. Their car sped quickly and Gavrilo and his group failed to act.

At the Town Hall, Mayor Curcic made a speech of welcome. Franz Ferdinand succumbed to anger and protested his violent reception to his luckless host. Sophie told her husband to be quiet. Presently, Franz Ferdinand's bloodstained script arrived and he recited its ironic thanks.

After this reception Sophie and Franz Ferdinand abandoned their schedules. At 1045 they climbed back into the Gräf und Stift to drive to visit the injured in hospital.

Meanwhile a disappointed Gavrilo had consoled himself with a sandwich and possibly a stiff drink in Schiller's Cafe on a corner at the Quay. In the confusion the Franz Ferdinand motorcade separated. Franz Ferdinand's driver, Leopold, reversed to rejoin the convoy. The backing car paused before Schiller's.

For a suspended moment all that could be heard in the shimmering morning heat was the soft susurration of the gathering foehn in the overhead wires, the clatter of the tappets and the gentle muffled phut of the exhaust.

In this interval, Gavrilo was astounded to recognise his intended victims. Gavrilo stepped from the shadows. He drew his FN1910 and shot Franz Ferdinand through the jugular. Firing again, he punctured Sophie's abdomen. The woman turned and fell on her knees before her bleeding husband with a prayer on her lips.

Gavrilo had forgotten his sacred duty to love without hate and to reverence the world and its creatures.

Franz Ferdinand died saying "Sophie, Sophie, don't die. Live for our children. My pain, it is nothing." Anton, a Jesuit priest, gave him his Last Rites. Sophie died ten minutes later.

The conspirators were arrested. The Austrian Police confiscated Gavrilo's weapon. The Belgian maker's mark disclosed that it was the property of Serbian Military Intelligence. But in any case, the conspirators had readily divulged their complicity with The Serbian Government.

Gavrilo was tried for high treason, but the Austrians did not hang him, for he was adjudged too young. He got twenty years.

So did Nedeljko. He apologised for the grenade attack at the Quay. Franz Ferdinand and Sophie's three young orphans, Sophie, Maximilian and Ernst, decided to exercise their sacred right to love without hate. They wrote Nedeljko a letter of forgiveness for his attempt on their parents' lives. All three of Franz Ferdinand and Sophie's children would spend World War Two in Dachau concentration camp.

Austria sent Serbia an ultimatum. If satisfied in full, Serbian independence would effectively extinguish. Serbia quibbled.

Austria mobilised its army as if to occupy the proud little Balkan state. Russia guaranteed Serbian independence and mobilised against Austria. Germany was obliged by treaty to defend Austria from any threat. Germany mobilised. Furthermore, Russia and France had secretly guaranteed Serbia at the inception of the statelet some forty years before. And France in turn guaranteed Russia, as was reciprocated.

When governments start guaranteeing things you know you are in trouble. When governments start guaranteeing each other you know trouble is a matter of time.

Now Germany's priority, as always, was to knock France out of a war and fight, if at all, on a single front. But the hills of the Vosges separate the two countries, and are a tough terrain. You do not want your troops beleaguered. The coastal plains of Flanders are a much softer and faster route to France.

Britain had guaranteed Belgian independence at the inception of the Belgian state in 1830. The Germans crossed Belgium. The British Empire declared war.

Soon a continent was in flames and a civilisation tottered. A fifty-year hemoclysm had commenced. In this first phase of it ten million died and 7.6 million disappeared without trace. Europe's race of horses was virtually exterminated and replaced with petrol engines. The Russians could not stand their losses. They called 47-year-old lawyer Vladimir from exile and he tried to take charge.

Russian emperor Nicolas asked his cousin George for shelter. He begged that at least his wife and children might have sanctuary. George promised rescue.

George was next in trouble. His country was resourceful but ill-led. Socialists were restive, feminists were burning property, and the Irish rose in open revolt. George felt his crown slipping. George reneged.

The Russians arrested their emperor Nicholas and his wife Alix, and, together with their five young children, and their loyal staff, murdered them. The Russians continued to fight each other. Five million died.

Germany was defeated and humiliated. In wrath a whole nation sought vengeance, and another fifty-five million died across a planet, thirteen million murdered in cold blood.

In the pages of his Inferno the poet Dante Alighieri had Satan take a man's love and turn it into a travesty of itself.

Franz Josef was a damaged man who loved.

All of the men we named were good men. They loved and lost. They loved the people around them and sought their happiness.

But they forgot The Will of God. They thought their ideas were best, and that honor, loyalty and intellect would suffice. They forgot their enemies were men, and also sought love. They forgot that their children must breed, and that the father is not the child. We shall remember them.

As my Late Mother used to say, "The road to Hell is paved with good intentions."

<u>Munchhausen's Syndrome by Proxy</u>

Females are extremely dangerous. Men attempt to develop social power through violence, a manifestation easily identified and managed. Women apply social power through solicitude, something much more subtle and difficult to counter. Ninety-seven percent of the unmasked perpetrators of Munchausen Syndrome By Proxy (MBP) are women.

I am not a clinician and I cannot improve upon the definitions and descriptions given by Dr Marc D Feldman in his 2024AD book "Playing Sick?" (ISBN 978-1-032-53364-3):-

In Munchausen by proxy (MBP), individuals create symptoms of illness not in themselves, but in dependent others who serve as "proxies". The majority of MBP perpetrators are women, most often mothers, who induce illness in their children or subject them to painful medical procedures in a quest for emotional satisfaction, such as attention from and control over others. MBP is a form of maltreatment (abuse and neglect), not mental disorder. The effect of MBP maltreatment on children who survive to adulthood is poignantly expressed in a first-hand account. This narrative reveals the profound confusion experienced by adult survivors in how to respond to legitimate illness and how to overcome feelings of shame and guilt for having been unwitting participants. Not surprisingly, some MBP children grow up to develop factitious disorder [self-destructive hypochondria].

(square-bracketed terms interpolated by JR Warren)
Feldman proceeds within the body of his Chapter Ten to clarify:-

The main types of [MBP] abuse are emotional, physical and sexual; neglect is categorized as physical or emotional. The permutations of maltreatment are innumerable, but include nutritional neglect, intentional drugging or poisoning (apart from MBP), neglect of necessary medical care, neglect of safety, educational neglect, and MBP itself. The types and subtypes overlap and intertwine in many cases. For instance, Julie Gregory, author of the book Sickened: The Memoir of a Munchausen by Proxy Childhood, [ISBN 978-0553803075] *was undoubtedly subjected to severe MBP. It incorporated medical abuse, social deprivation, nutritional neglect and medical neglect (The last was manifested by her mother's delaying badly needed treatment for authentic maladies.). Physical abuse in the form of beatings and emotional abuse through her mother's constantly shaming her and hurling outrageous accusations occurred as well but was usually independent of the MBP.*

I do not wish to disgust or distress my reader but the gamut of MBP can and does include burns, scalds and cuts explained as accidents, as well as the induction of gastro-intestinal trauma and genital mutilation, the latter passed-off as religious observance.

<u>Homosexuality</u>

Procreative copulation is a Divine consummation devoutly to be desired.

The test of sin is that it tends to diminish the viability of the species or it reduces the probability of the survival of existing individuals.

We can say that sin is *non-conducive* in the sense that it diverts fertility from its procreative path.

Accordingly, we may rationally think that masturbation and any activity that deposits the Seed of Life in the digestive tract is sinful, and in the latter case besides primary waste the act may induce the spread of disease.

Whilst abortion or any murder is obviously sinful I do not preclude contraception because the reasoned suspension of fertility conduces to the larger conservation of mankind and its resources, whilst abstinence risks greater spiritual perils even than sexual promiscuity.

Do not mistake my meaning: Few things are more sublime than the *chaste* love of two men for one another, or indeed the chaste love of two women.

I am a seventy-three year-old Englishman and I think you will understand the horror with which men like me view male homosexuality and its, for us, inescapable connotation of buggery.

On the afternoon of 15th of May 2025 I boarded a bus in Chasetown which was soon alive with students who had recently adjourned the Erasmus Darwin Academy, a day high school. A boy took an aisle seat a knight's move in front of me. Presently another lad, also about fifteen or sixteen, stood before him with the angelic smile of a besotted maiden. The sitting youth gestured to grab his friend's buttocks, but did not actually make contact. I was compellingly reminded of the strangely epicene non-contacting wrestlers of Nazi sculpture.

You are entitled to dismiss this shameless exhibition as an endearing manifestation of immature love out of which you hope the boys may grow. After all, many adolescents pass through a homosexual stage. I did, though I was free of the instinct by the time I was eleven. Love is a continuum, it evolves and occults like the phases of the Moon, and is not necessarily evil.

Homosexually is a psychoneurosis, one of a myriad expressions of such, and, properly suppressed, is not necessarily more hazardous than nail-biting.

None admonished the two lads, nor should they have been parted by others. Such repression may have been more destructive than the offence. The correct response is prayer, and I hope that the two lads remain lifelong friends, but marry loved women who bear them happy and healthy children.

Human Sacrifice

The story of The Bible is the narrative of the Ancient Semitic peoples' struggle with the evil of human sacrifice, and especially the immolation of children, a feature of Semitic worship in both Palestine and Phoenicia, before the Romans suppressed this baleful rite forever.

1 And it came to pass after these things, that God did tempt Abraham, and said unto him, Abraham: and he said, Behold, here I am.

2 And he said, Take now thy son, thine only son Isaac, whom thou lovest, and get thee into the land of Moriah; and offer him there for a burnt offering upon one of the mountains which I will tell thee of.

3 And Abraham rose up early in the morning, and saddled his ass, and took two of his young men with him, and Isaac his son, and clave the wood for the burnt offering, and rose up, and went unto the place of which God had told him.

4 Then on the third day Abraham lifted up his eyes, and saw the place afar off.

5 And Abraham said unto his young men, Abide ye here with the ass; and I and the lad will go yonder and worship, and come again to you.

6 And Abraham took the wood of the burnt offering, and laid it upon Isaac his son; and he took the fire in his hand, and a knife; and they went both of them together.

7 And Isaac spake unto Abraham his father, and said, My father: and he said, Here am I, my son. And he said, Behold the fire and the wood: but where is the lamb for a burnt offering?

8 And Abraham said, My son, God will provide himself a lamb for a burnt offering: so they went both of them together.

9 And they came to the place which God had told him of; and Abraham built an altar there, and laid the wood in order, and bound Isaac his son, and laid him on the altar upon the wood.

10 And Abraham stretched forth his hand, and took the knife to slay his son.

11 And the angel of the LORD called unto him out of heaven, and said, Abraham, Abraham: and he said, Here am I.

12 And he said, Lay not thine hand upon the lad, neither do thou any thing unto him: for now I know that thou fearest God, seeing thou hast not withheld thy son, thine only son from me.

(Genesis 22:1-12)

The New Testament culminates with the Crucifixion of Christ, the Sacrifice of the Lamb of God, with which lethal sacrifice ceased in civilised communities.

The True Sacrifice is the sacrifice of the self, and selfish desires, including the unrighteous aspects of self-magnification.

In 922AD, Ibn Fadlan, an envoy of the Caliph of Baghdad found himself with merchants beside the River Volga, where he witnessed a Viking Funeral:-

…When one of their chiefs dies, his family asks his girls and pages, "Which one of you will die with him?" Then one of them answers, "I." From the time that he utters this word, he is no longer free: should he wish to draw back, he is not permitted. For the most part, however, it is the girls that offer themselves. So, when the man of whom I spoke died, they asked his girls, "Who will die with him?" One of them answered, "I." She was then committed to two girls, who were to keep watch over her, accompany her wherever she went, and even, on occasion, wash her feet…

…During the whole of this period, the girl gave herself over to drinking, and singing, and was cheerful and gay…

…The girl who had devoted herself to death meanwhile walked to and fro, entering one after another of the tents which they had there. The occupant of each tent lay with her saying, [to the girl] "Tell your master 'I did this only for love of you.'"…

The sacrificial girl was then escorted to the Ship of Immolation with a crone, as it were an officiant, a high priestess of execution called the Angel of Death.

Ibn Fadlan's narrative resumes:-

…Here she took off her two bracelets, and gave them to the old woman who was called the angel of death, and who was to murder her. She also drew off her two anklets, and passed them to the two serving-maids, who were the daughters of the so called angel of death. Then they lifted her into the ship, but did not yet admit her to the tent. Now men came up with shields and staves, and handed her a cup of strong drink. This she took, sang over it, and emptied it. 'With this', so the interpreter told me, 'she is taking leave of those who are dear to her.' Then another cup was handed her, which she also took, and began a lengthy song. The crone admonished her to drain the cup without lingering, and to enter the tent where her master lay. By this time, as it seemed to me, the girl had become dazed; she made as though she would enter the tent and the ship, when the hag seized her by the head, and dragged her in. At this moment the men began to beat upon their shields with the staves, in order to drown the noise of her outcries, which might have terrified the other girls, and deterred them from seeking death with their masters in the future. Then six men entered into the tent, and each and every one had carnal companionship with her. Then they laid her down by her master's side, while two of the men seized her by the feet, and two by the hands. The old woman known as the angel of death now knotted a rope around her neck, and handed the ends to two of the men to pull. Then with a broad-bladed dagger she smote her between the ribs, and drew the blade forth, while the two men strangled her with the rope till she died…"

The mortuary ship was then ignited.

The astonishing thing about this relation, apart from the measured stateliness of the English prose, is the volition of the victim and the barbaric prestige of her person.

These and other remarkable features seem to post-figure the Gospel narratives that culminate in the Crucifixion of Christ.

But all such tales are ancient stories, emblematic of a timeless anthropology, for if we should meet God then we, reader, are the Sacrifice.

AOT
WARREN

CHAPTER FOUR
HOLY CORRECTION

Beating the Bounds

There exists in England a most ancient custom in which priests pace the boundary of a parish or some old precinct in the company of boys, always natives of the vicinage and usually of magisterial class.

When the party encounter a boundary marker stone, or perhaps a tree, or some other obvious but corruptible terminal, the company pauses to pray and the lads are invited to lower their trousers to receive a memorable swipe with a birch switch. It is desired that the boys remember forever the limits of their territory, lest mistakenly they resort to resolve a dispute with their neighbours by sword and fire. If the boys weep they are consoled with copper coins and cakes and ale, and of the food and drink the men partake also.

In the best walks, the members of the opposite preserve concur with the first company upon their side of the frontier, and concur in a like manner.

The intent was never to harm the boys, very far from it, or even to hurt them, but to make them remember forever, as if by repetition, the lawful limits of their portion.

This is a Holy Rogation, performed at Rogationtide, and not more often than every three years. At Rogation God is asked to remit his anger at us and to protect us from disaster. God is asked to help us husband the bounty of the land, to make sure that those who lack share that bounty, and that we gloat not in our good fortune, for we curate the land, not own the land. It is as I say a very ancient custom: Roman, originally pagan, though we no longer sacrifice dogs, sacred to the Ancients almost everywhere, and of course birching boys is rightly highly illegal across Europe.

Notwithstanding that, Beating the Bounds is special.

Peace is a fruitful future. Asking God for peace is special. Peace is special. So is God.

The field of human relations and the agreed boundaries of personal integrities and behaviours is also a champion country. The markers of the march are moveable. Overtly or covertly.

There are, as it were, no limes of natural topography such as ridges or rivers, only the Word of God and maybe the isolated signpost to navigate the fecund waste.

Is it better that the bounds are beaten or that the borderlands go to the transgressor strongest of arm, settled literally upon the field of dishonor?

The Principles of Occasion and Consent

Beating the bounds exemplifies two of the principal problems that dog the application of tonic chastisements, that is to say beatings intended to benefit the recipient *only* with indirect benefits, if any, to the second and third parties.

Chastisement should only be used very sparingly at irregular intervals of time when the circumstances truly warrant it, and there is genuine reason to think that life will get worse *for the recipient* if corporal correction is evaded. There should be nothing timetabled, predictable or tariffed about it. Schedules are inevitably for the convenience of those who administer, not those who receive. Schedules and tariffs give the poor recipient plenty of time for anxiety and terror of anticipation, knowing that he who beats him will conform to an inflexible program. Once parameterised, chastisement should be prompt and supportive, not delayed and corrosive. Correction should be just that: Something helpful and guiding, not something spiteful or vengeful. For sure, bounds-beatings are scheduled for every third Rogationtide, and there are of course chorologically-fixed stations at which the rite is performed. But otherwise than that acts and observances are fluid with plenty of room for discretion and forbearance, including cheerful bribery.

If we intend to correct a Penitent or a spouse we should agree not a *tariff* but a *list* of transgressions that render the subject eligible. For example, we may agree that any breach of a Commandment of God is potentially subject to discipline, supplemented perhaps by specification of actions which jeopardise the safety and security of others or the subject himself. Petty failings, insufficiencies or honest errors should explicitly be ineligible for corporal correction.

Consent is another complex issue, clouded by the concept of "non-consensual consent". Fortunately for us, Correctional Penance has clear-cut consensual characteristics. By definition, the Penitent would not present in the sanctuary unless he was prepared to engage the known strictures of his Holy Correction, including any spankings handed down. Paradoxically, another guarantee of genuine informed consent is the extreme secrecy of the fact and content of the confessional. That extreme secrecy renders virtually impossible any social pressure by third parties. Thirdly, the operation of a safeword protocol also certifies the currency of consent. And since in Holy Correction a Penitent is never restrained, simple roll-clear is possible *in extremis*.

Forgive an apparent digression, but the problem of consent is less clear-cut in the case of marital spanking customs. For example, consider my case. I am a married man. To the best of my understanding, I agreed to love, honor and protect my Wife, and she agreed to love, honor, and obey me. I also swore to honor her with my body, and she reciprocated. Never mind that both of us are aged, ill and incapable. Never mind that the form of words at the ceremony was almost certainly variant: My contract is not with Camden Metropolitan Borough Council, and it most definitely is not with The Home Office (the UK police ministry). My Contract is with God in Person. Accordingly, if I break my Contract with God I consider myself justly eligible for one of three things: A hiding from my Wife; divorce; or Damnation. Of these only the first would be proportionate to run-of-the-mill offences. Marital vows are the classic example *par excellence* of "non-consensual consent".

Because my contract is with God, if I tell my Wife to spank me every Thursday evening (except on polling days) I am blaspheming a Holy Sacrament. Equally, if I make my Wife sign a consent form before spanking her, then I am not merely insulting, officious and oppressive (as well as cowardly): I am also blaspheming a Holy Sacrament.

With regard to Beating the Bounds there is also ambiguity surrounding consent. For certain, no one ever asked the lads at the sharp end if they consented to the ritual. But it is equally sure that the father of any eligible boy would consider himself mortally affronted if his son was excluded from the rite, as would any boy old enough to understand the implication. None of the presiding priests would have been challenged to settle matters on the field of honor, but nevertheless local magistrates would have had abundant means of avenging themselves on any cleric so presumptuous. And as we have seen elsewhere, the beating priests were very solicitous to mollify any lad who became over-emotional during the walk, and not just by lightening their strokes. Is this another example of "non-consensual consent"?

<u>Spanking</u>

The Life of the Spirit is a continuum. The line between Whoredom and Prophesy is invisible and its exact location uncharted. Good people have trespassed the frontier since the day of Eve and, doubtless, before. A compass is useless at the poles.

Spanking is a serious matter. Since earliest childhood I suffered a neurotic horror and disgust of the custom, but also occasional fascination. I have been spanked. As my earthly life draws to its close I lay some ghosts. The progress of dying has other advantages. I less often seek to impress, and I am less jealous of my reputation.

Fifty-five percent of English men and women express an interest in spanking or think they might enjoy it. The British Labour Party and feminists have considered its suppression but appear to realise the task is hopeless, so engrained is the tradition and so beguiling illicit delights. The worst excesses have fallen under European interdict. The behaviour is also widespread in the USA and other anglocentric cultures, though innate and a feature of all societies.

It is easy to smile, but spanking is a serious issue. It is easy enough to contemplate as fantasy or at the level of existential literature. Execution in the life is another matter. If you submit to Correctional spanking you might enjoy remarkable pleasure but will suffer greatly. And I am not talking about a sore bottom.

For years men have struggled to mean what they say and say what they mean. If you find these pages offensive then I most sincerely apologise. I understand your view though I consider it inappropriate to the occasion. This is not about depravity, violence or subjugation. It is about love, trust and forgiveness.

In this disquisition spanking is exclusively the act of striking a person on one or both nates with the flat of the hand. According to British usage, instruments are never applied: That would be whipping, something quite other. Hand spanking leaves no physical mark or injury upon a healthy adult, but is potentially very painful, and should also cause pain to the person who spanks.

Spanking is a chastisement, specifically, in the religious sense, a castigation.

We wish to use spanking only to correct sentiment not to deter behaviour, and very definitely never to punish or avenge. And we wish to use it only as an adjunct to sacramental penance.

Religious spanking is always consensual.

Spanking is a psychosexual activity, though participation between same-sex celebrants is not necessarily homosexual. Never apply spanking to children or adolescents. It induces lasting sadism or masochism or both.

Always honour your Penitent. He or she should wholly be bare under God, and so should his Confessor, if the Penitent consents. Never admonish your Penitent, or imply disgust at his body or his crimes. Always build: Never strike down. And of course, unless you are a demon, you will never mock.

A First Look at Correctional Spanking

Correctional Spanking Therapy is a harsh and kind activity that fortifies us better to prosecute our brief but vital tryst with the heroic and the ridiculous.

Of course the method is an artificial re-direction of evolved and delicately-balanced mechanisms but is a means to an end, does not compromise primary functionalities, and the end may have both intrinsic and survival benefits that outweigh the risks taken. Everything in life is a risk. It is sad that most of our risks are pointless and their outcomes often tragic. Our method is bizarre. But our risk is not pointless. And its outcome could be wondrous to behold.

Correctional Spanking Therapy is indeed therapy. It is possible to benefit from it purely as a form of psychoanalytic consultation, and some psychiatrists employ it in this wholly secular mode. The sacrament of Holy Correction is quite different. In Correction you celebrate your subjection to God and ask him to make you the person He wants you to be. In the presence of faith the two processes converge with immense power.

Do not mistake my meaning. I do not imply that a few cuffs on the bottom are in any way a natural justice retribution for the pain and harm you have caused. Certainly, a thousand blows would not repay me for my crimes. It is easy for you and I to think of it as punishment, but that is wrong. Rather it is a small but felt penance for your sin, a mark of your contrition, and a rite of passage to a higher frame of mind in which you contemplate your wickedness and your plans to destroy it. It is more like discipline than punishment in the sense that it conditions and encourages us to better future conduct.

Correctional spanking has no attritive value even when taken, literally, as part of a calorie-controlled diet. For the Sin of Gluttony, by example, is too subtle for deterrence, though appreciation of a sin's ethical ramifications can mitigate or terminate its future course.

For sure, it is the prayer or the confession that is morally efficacious, but even that is too forgettable, even the sin licenced, if the wrong confessed is speciously absolved with empty ritual. Sin is harmful and should hurt, even at a token level. Not as punishment but as tonic. Remember: The real price is paid by someone else.

Please read this work in its entirety.

There is intentional repetition, paraphrase and pleonasm.

Any paradox perceived arises from our existential condition.

Holy Correction

Holy Correction is a religious Sacrament: Confession followed by Penance. The Penance need not of course involve spanking though many find spanking brief, convenient and salutary.

I need to emphasis at this outset that Holy Correction has nothing to do with Christian Domestic Discipline (CDD) or with Loving Domestic Discipline (LDD). CDD and LDD subject only the wife of a marriage who consents to be spanked by her husband whenever he adjudges her deserving, and permission once given is irrevocable. For Holy Correction, any consenting and competent adult is eligible to confess sin and experience due castigation or other penance *in the meantime only* for the Sacrament to complete. Therefore, Holy Correction is in this aspect comparable to Holy Communion (eucharist) with which it may readily be integrated. Holy Correction is about the free and consensual atonement for sin and the contrite assuagement of guilt and shame in the Blessing of God, often with earthly restitution to follow.

When spanked, Holy Correction is a rather conservative but effective form of Correctional Spanking Therapy (CST). It involves admitting personal acts of wickedness, prayer, light castigation, further prayer or reading, and finding practical ways to improve behaviour.

It is a sacred but not a solemn act, grounded in cheerful friendship, and adapted to the needs of modern people.

I should further emphasise that potentially anyone can benefit from CST or even Holy Correction, not just practicing Christians.

Holy Correctional spanking is not about humiliation, control or infantilisation, and most definitely coercion has no rôle in it. Certainly, for an hour or two one will be treated like a child of olden times with cuddles, praise, prayers, smacks and Scripture lessons. But any CST is about building one's self-confidence and happiness as a more-than-effective adult; enhancing your authority in the home, workplace and community; and helping you project your skills as a humane but decisive contributor to the reconstruction of our nations and our neighborhoods.

Correctional spanking is fully consensual. It is a demanding and draining athletic ascetic exercise, and requires reasonable physical fitness. It should never be attempted after taking alcohol or psychoactive medication, and smoking should be avoided before a session. The process alters breathing and heart rates, and interruptions may be necessary for breathing exercises. Any devout and empathetic man or woman can be a Confessor, but he cannot confess anyone under eighteen or someone who in his opinion is likely to be imperilled by, or unable to benefit from, CST at the time of presentation.

Like rugby, ordinary CST involves intimate, but not sexual, physical contact. But unlike rugby Holy Correction involves sacred observances before God. Also like rugby, it beats drug therapies hands down, if you will forgive my expression.

In Holy Correction, it is essential that confessor and penitent trust and value one another absolutely. This is not too difficult for certain kinds of familiar religious people, but very difficult for strangers in our broken society. There must be informed consent before a finger is laid on the Penitent, and most especially a confessor must know that confession is the Penitent's sincere, free and individual choice, and not a reluctant accession to pressure from others. Anything one says to the confessor is absolutely confidential, though a Penitent is welcome to share prayers or advice with others.

<u>Nakedness</u>

There are many practical, psychological and spiritual reasons for unclothed Correctional Penance and it is a very old tradition. Your nakedness is neither an insult nor a humiliation, and is not intended to be such. Your nakedness is an earnest of your good faith. Your nakedness is part of the reality of your natural state of godliness that the process of Correction develops and discloses.

Striking someone over their clothing exposes them to unnecessary danger. The striker's aim and accuracy are compromised, and so is his grip. Clothing fibers and microbes are driven into the skin leading at best to irritation and at worst to topical sepsis. Resistance is encouraged and this leads to dangerous mis-strikes and possible organ damage. If the penitent's skin is exposed it is much easier to perceive early signs of arousal or distress and to adjust or suspend the physical aspects of Correction for both the safety and comfort of the subject. Sweat and other secretions can be gently wiped away allowing the penitent to keep his mind focused upon his corrections and his devotions without fretting over distracting incidental discomforts. And of course rubbing or massage are impossible if the subject is clothed.

Your Confessor will make sure to strip him or herself of everything sharp or metallic from his body and his clothing, including but not limited to his wristwatch, bangles, rings (

including his wedding band), hairgrips and obviously ear-rings and other piercings.

He will bare his feet and trim his finger and toe nails.

Rather than wearing shorts and vest or a petticoat it is better he be clothed in nightwear, and best of all that he or she works naked if you the Penitent will permit it.

The room is warm enough to be inhabited naked in comfort but sweating can induce chill. So after a Reparation a duvet or other smooth cover may be necessary during Restoration, or you may bring a dressing gown of smooth fabric.

Being naked enhances the Penitent's feeling of vulnerability and his willingness to submit to correction, and to accept the mental and spiritual benefits brought.

If nothing physical is hidden he or she senses by instinct that deceit and concealment are difficult if not impossible: The Penitent knows all is transparent to God whatever, and that his Confessor is also paying close attention.

A word if you are concerned about decency. Your nakedness is total and your decency also. You would not quail at being bathed by a nurse or massaged by a sports masseur. Neither would you think twice, upon a beach in France, of stripping for a swim. What is highly indecent is this corporal act if you are costumed, even if wearing street clothes or underwear only.

Be assured, especially if you are female, that there is nothing shameful about lying naked in a man's lap, or even enjoying the idea: The shame inheres in the wickedness that brought you to this position.

If you are a woman I say this: I am a man. Your nakedness will almost certainly arouse me. Your mere presence may well do so. I may not be able to resist the temptation to remark upon your beauty, but I will never make any lewd comment or invitation. Wiping, rubbing or ointment application may be intimate, but you will never indecently be touched, unless, of course, we are married!

If you lie naked in my lap you at once feel very vulnerable and utterly secure. If I am a male and you a female, then my natural instinct is to protect you and you know that whilst you are borne in my hands nothing and no-one will be allowed to harm you.

It is impossible for me not to feel compassion for some creature lying naked in my power. I shall be restrained and my blows reluctant. And that is as it should be.

Occasionally, the position or the beating may cause arousal.

Ethologists might tell us that this is a textbook simian dominance-submission response evolved to maximise the probability of procreation. In the very different and equally true idiom of Genesis Chapter One God Created his living things by the Fifth Day and issued his first injunction: "Be fruitful, and multiply".

Your delight in sex is a Gift from God. Be not ashamed. It is not sin.

Your nakedness recalls the State of Innocency in which God Created Man and Woman. It reminds you of the state in which you delimit your mortal life, and it prefigures the Innocence you shall resume.

CHAPTER FIVE
OBJECTIONS

To those who are concerned about mis-placed Metaphor I say this:

Metaphor inheres in most, or arguably all, human writings, because even the most gifted of us struggle to represent the world as it is. Our language and the thought its predicate is a dull mirror of the emanations of God's Thought. Even Holy Scripture can be read as Letter or as Metaphor, or indeed as both simultaneously. Without I hope presumption or offense I believe that Scripture should be interpreted as both letter and metaphor. No-one objects to Plato or Virgil and calls either unedifying because they are metaphorical, or rejects Plutarch's or Pliny's lessons because they are literal. The vast bulk of my own sorry works concern narrowly-defined scientific or technical issues treated in a highly literal empirical manner but using extensive mathematical methods. And yet mathematics is solely a symbolic metaphor, with no essential relation to these natural problems: Which problems would, however, be humanly intractable without mathematics. It is not for nothing that the old ones called metaphor "figure".

What follows is obviously executable in the life as a literality, but may nevertheless have metaphorical overtones, and be read as metaphor. It is difficult for me to think of anything cruder than a simian dominance-submission ritual, or more sublime than sacramental love.

To those who worry about Obscenity I say this:

For certain, spanking carries an inescapable sexual undertone. This is one reason why it must never be applied to children or adolescents (it induces life-long sadomasochism). I was spanked. I am a sadomasochist. Because of its sexual loading it is also congenial, though not essential, that the two participants are of opposite sexes. We should remember that the first injunction of the Creator was that we should procreate and he appointed the enjoyment of sex to encourage that. And if you object to the image rather than the act, then which part of any living creature, Designed by God, can possibly be obscene? We are discussing an act of love, whether prosecuted by spouses or strangers, a very intimate act of firmness and forbearance.

Beyond the obvious, nothing is done to hurt the penitent. His shortcomings, freely confessed, are not reprimanded, or lectured about, or harped upon. Neither are they mocked or trivialised, no matter how risible or irrelevant they might seem to us. This is an act of trust. This is only about magnifying the man or woman under our hand. This is about restoring a person's good opinion of himself in the Eyes of God, restoring his self-respect and self-confidence, that he may confront his past, offer reparation and repentance, and move forward in strength. It is especially not corporal punishment, an abomination, though it bears a superficial resemblance to such.

Beyond a few harmless slaps, which may or may not be offered, we give the penitent flesh-to-flesh contact; prayers; cool water to drink; a few kind words, dwelling upon his known or apparent strengths and virtues; morsels of bread and wine; and a valedictory kiss and cuddle, if not also a soothing bath and a square meal. Always and only kindness, physical warmth, a soft word and a smile, security and respect. A quiet prayer or parable, perhaps *ad hominem* or *ad mulierum*, but never accusatory or censorious.

And if gentle violence is not acceptable, the participants can arrange alternative penances, such as acts of charity to man or beast, or even simple chores, because these can be as or more valuable to a devout and contrite spirit. Most penitents would be habituated to such anyway. But most men and almost all women would prefer as well or instead a concise, cleansing and condign exercise, rigorous and restorative, sharp and short, humbling but not humiliating, and marking a memorable boundary between their old corruptions and their new recoveries.

To those who object in the name of Justice I say this:

No Justice is achievable in our Fallen world, because our knowledge is imperfect, our judgment defective, and our wickedness inherent. In any case it should be obvious that Justice can never be served by hitting someone on the bottom, whether in metaphor or in actuality. Satan promises us Justice in the next life: Christ promised us Mercy, and stood his Father guarantor. You can always grant mercy and endow it now: Even, and this is another profound paradox, by force. You cannot confer justice. If you have a murderer, a slaver, an infanticide or a procuress on your lap, what justice can you confer? Your lips are sealed, not least because the State is incapable of justice also. You can only do what you can for their immortal spirits, and if you are very lucky (or very skilful) you will make another John Newton. On the other hand, what are you going to do with the woman who locked her husband out of a shared hotel room, or who reports that she swore at a cyclist: Laugh? There is a special gallery of Hell for the mockers and the sneerers. Now that is metaphor, of course. But mock or sneer and see if I am right.

Our only just response is love.

And the only important outcome (apart, we hope from a distinct improvement in behaviour) is that the Penitent walks away thinking and feeling that he has paid the fair price for his sin, whatever it was. Our concern is with his benefit. His courage has engendered his Act of Trust. He trusted you. He also trusted God.

To those who object to my Infelicities of expression I say this:

I apologise for my many tautologies and antitheses, for my shifts of tense, for my numerous vulgarities and Briticisms, and lapses of syntax and semantics. I find it very difficult to express myself, especially about a matter at once so very important, and yet, in a certain curious manner, so very commonplace. I have taken many years to hone this text, based on seventy-three of considering this matter closely, often too closely. I should say that I use the term "spank" in its UK sense as to strike someone on the nates with the flat of the hand, rather than the US sense of to strike there with a chosen instrument. This disquisition is about spiritual enlightenment, not torture. My literary style is very conservative. I do not apologise for that. I write in the barely-gendered English language. As in all my writings, the masculine includes the feminine, except in contexts where distinction of sex is necessary and manifest.

There is intentional repetition, paraphrase and pleonasm.

The subject of this disquisition lies at the intersection of sex, violence and religion, all three controversial subjects in their own right. This text has progressed through around fifty major revisions. I am confident that significant flaws remain. I have tried very hard to avoid giving unnecessary offence, to avoid giving encouragement to malign people and to avoid salaciousness. I have included a few very offensive words to show where and why they should not be used. I want to think of myself as a Christian and as a scientist, not as a pornographer or a blasphemer. We have to admit that spanking is a very disturbing subject. So is religion. Both religion and spanking should disturb. If you are not disturbed by "Acts of Trust" then I have wasted your time and helped you in no manner. If I have wasted your time or offended you I humbly apologise.

CHAPTER SIX
PROCEDURE AND EXPERIENCE

<u>Some Dangers of Ritual Violence</u>

When you peruse the existing literature upon spanking, both in print and on the Internet, certain facts rapidly manifest. Well over ninety-percent of it is of a pornographic character, more or less frank and more or less well-spoken. This of itself should convince of their error those who believe or affect to believe that spanking is non-sexual. Notorious national traditions are clearly visible, ranging from the laughable and the playful, through the meretricious and the banal, to the disfiguring and the torturous.

I am not qualified to assess the psychological or clinical aspects of spanking very far beyond the superficial aspects of endocrinal response but I should make a few remarks about the addictive habituation that is a hazard with regard to any intense pleasure from smoking to religious ecstasy and virtually anything in between.

There is real psycho-spiritual danger in frequent participation in spanking, whether as spanker or the person spanked, the so-called spankee.

This danger is exemplified by married couples and others who embrace the Christian Domestic Discipline (CDD) or Loving Domestic Discipline (LDD) lifestyles, or similar customs. Some of these speak of very frequent beatings, almost exclusively borne by the women, wives or daughters, and even of weekly or other scheduled "maintenance spankings". Many speak of punishments for very trivial or even non-existent infractions or "just so" spankings. In my assessment, this is sadism and masochism lent a veneer of religious respectability, and sometimes with a specious Biblical validation in terms of the Pauline Epistles or something. I am not a prude. If a couple are excited by such things and it helps them to fulfil their natural vocation then I am all for it. For sure, Paul exhorts men to love their wives and women to obey their husbands but nowhere in the New Testament is corporal punishment adverted to, except as an act of mockery or oppression. If we approve spankings it is solely as an act of the deepest and most humble respect, especially on the part of the spanker. Many couples see the act as a decisive event that clears the air, neutralises all grievances, re-sets history and history's trajectory, and permits a relationship to move forward happily and constructively in enhanced love and respect on both sides. In my opinion, this is the healthy attitude to take to spankings.

By the way, none of this has any relevancy to feminism, equal rights, domestic abuse, or any other political or forensic consideration. Our observations are purely about religious observance and whether or not social violence has a role in such.

Whilst we are on the subject of CDD a word to its practitioners about bedtime. Never appoint bedtime for the administration of a spanking, routine or occasional. Certainly your wife should lie naked in your arms but a Christian bedtime should be something like this: Voice a brief prayer over your wife (not *for your wife*; for something you know will delight her, animals, world peace, a safe journey tomorrow, the kids, even just a good night's sleep); then a kiss; if she asks you to father her child, then lovingly and procreatively endow her with the Seed of Life that God entrusted to you; then ask her if she wants anything before she sleeps (a cup of cocoa, two aspirins and a Jaffa cake, time to pray, her nightdress); then another kiss and a good night.

Vary it.

Ritual can too easily degenerate to pantomime.

Satan wants you to make a travesty of your love. Satan wants you to reduce your habits of charity and Christian piety to cruelty and mummery. Satan wants you to lapse into pessimism, cynicism, atheism, ennui and self-indulgence. Only then can Satan make you the evil person He wants you to be.

Good people are unselfish, forgiving and supportive. They never gloat in ascendancy, or seek an unshared gratification. They never lecture or sermonise at transgressors. An adult knows the nature of his or her offence, and has assessed its gravity uninstructed. A man or woman may ask an erring spouse to read back to him a relevant verse or two of Scripture. Even that is rarely necessary. Grown-ups know where they stand, and why. A man or woman asks the sinning spouse quietly, courteously, even reverently to disrobe, never shouting, never criticising, never censuring. People of quality should never shout, swear or threaten. Neither should they "answer back" as we say in Britain. Often, the state of nakedness is sufficient of itself to urge contrition and apology. In such a case, no further action is required, beyond maybe an embrace, a kiss, and a word of thanks. Otherwise the offender is gently but firmly taken in hand. The sinner gets what he needs and no more. Good people err on the side of clemency.

When Christians marry both the man and the woman vow to honor each other with their bodies; and, at least of the spirit, if no longer the letter of the law, the man promises to love, honour and protect, whilst the woman promises to love, honor and obey. The man must protect the woman *even against herself,* and the woman must obey the man *in all godly things.*

For example, a man is entitled to take effective action to prevent his wife smoking, over-eating or biting her nails, though of course in modern life we generally prefer persuasion or clinical methods to any more primeval recourse. On the other hand if a man orders his wife to steal, kill or commit adultery, or otherwise defy God, then the woman has a *right and duty* to refuse.

For example, a man says to his wife: "Your mother is a cow." The wife should reply: "No she is not. You should honor my parent just as you honor your own." I should explain for readers confused by this very British and in the UK very usual scenario that though a literal cow is a pleasant animal, the use of the word in the given context is highly derogatory.

If, though, the man says the couple will vacation in a caravan at Skegness this year, though his wife is set upon a week's shopping in New York, then the woman should defer without complaint and ideally without betraying any displeasure, if she has sufficient self-control. The man is the Head of the family but should have the common sense, and the self-confidence, to behave flexibly. A man who is able will console his woman with tender love. It is not the man who is dominant and the woman submissive: In a Christian marriage, properly managed and lovingly husbanded, the real submissive who is subjugated is Satan.

These customs and attitudes have the virtue of preserving a loving and harmonious relationship to the safety and nurturing of any children. But these customs and attitudes are valuable whatever, even in sad childless marriages.

Spats, arguments, rancour, spite and worse are suppressed, and the pleasure and security of all involved maximised.

To be specific, reasonable castigation is only justified against either partner if they defy a Commandment of God or act against *their own* physical or spiritual integrity to the peril of the marriage. Habitual beatings are abusive even when consensual: It is possible to abuse oneself. So are chastisements that are excessive, or which leave permanent injuries. If the man or woman threatens suicide or other serious self-harm, do not beat him, instead seek urgent medical intervention.

We should always keep a sense of proportion and a sense of humor, even in matters of sex, violence and religion. Or did I mean *especially* in matters of sex, violence and religion?

The total number of US marriages that have ended in divorce is around 45 percent: The total number of US CDD and LDD marriages that have ended in divorce is about five percent of such marriages. The total number of UK marriages that have ended in divorce is about 42%: The number of DD UK marriages that have so ended is not known.

I apologise to those who have found tedious what they may consider an irrelevant digression. I reason that these matrimonial chastisement customs may have a paradigmatic bearing upon Correctional Spanking in that you may expect certain enthusiasts to abuse the facility, especially by over-attendance or trivialisation. Trivialisation will prove especially problematic when you are asked to confess peccadillos that you feel are wasting your time and money, but which are genuinely distressing to your prospective Penitent. You may search in vain for the relevant Authority. You may be tempted to question his or her motivation. It is not easy. But if it were you would not be interested and you certainly would not be reading this. I very much think that a sacramental observance should be a spontaneous but very special occasion, not like a trip to the cinema or even to the dentist. Matrimonial chastisement may also have a paradigmatic bearing on confessional practices in that both parties to that should, so far is appropriate and practicable, emulate the mutual respect and tender prayerful regard of the well-adjusted couple.

<u>The Penitent</u>

If you are so much as considering Correctional penance you are a courageous and original-minded person. You are important. Even if you think you are alone and bereft upon Earth you are desperately Loved by Someone watching. I reverence your will to become a better person. If you fall into my hands I shall cherish you and do my very best to nurture your Immortal Spirit.

There is no wickedness so heinous or depraved that you may not bring it to The Feet of God, that He may take it from you, annihilate it and restore to you the Innocence that it adulterated. Neither is there a sin so small or niggling that it cannot be searched out and banished.

Your Confession is deeply, utterly sacred. It is really something for God's Ears alone, but any man who might hear your Prayer is vastly privileged and is compelled, even against his inclination, devoutly to wish your Forgiveness from God and from all.

A special word if you are an atheist. Confess to a trusted friend by all means. It is always good for you and yours, even if you cannot yet believe, and even if my methods and myself are unacceptable to you. But I would really welcome you. You cannot imagine what it would be like for me to hear your first prayer. I wept just to think about it. And nearly ten years later, I weep again.

<u>If You Cannot Believe</u>

If you are not a believer the act of confession is still good for you: Psychologically, emotionally and, yes, spiritually. Just as importantly it prepares you to take steps to make your future life kinder and fairer to others.

I understand and respect your doubt. I was an atheist for most of my life and I know what it feels like, and the many and diverse considerations that commend the view. When you rest on my lap you will get no lectures or proselytisation: Such would be most irreligious of me. I know that you respect my belief or otherwise you would not find yourself in such a position.

God loves you even if you do not think he exists. If you had a son or daughter and he thought he was the biological issue of another person, would you love him the less? God loves you because you are his creature. Your intellectual position is part of the Expression of His own Personality. He will adjust your position when He is ready. That could be tomorrow or in several billion years' time, but it will happen. You are important to Him.

You may think I have contradicted my own belief in Free Will. I do not pretend to comprehend the Mind of God, but I do know, and have for some forty-two years, that our human logical apparatus is irredeemably flawed. Cleverer men than I have known that since 1934 at the latest.

If you are a believer and you are reading this, do not worry for atheists or other non-Christians. They will not be tortured after they are dead. Their condition denies them full enjoyment of God's Love, but He will always do what He can to delight them with good things. They are in God's Hands and he will redeem them, and His larger Pledge.

If you are not a believer you will suffer no disadvantage, nor enjoy any privilege, during any Correction I facilitate. I acknowledge that you will not be able to pray. But I will pray for you and I will read to you any edifying literature that you require. You may read to me without your motives being mistaken. I will do my best to make sure that you take wholesome enjoyment of your Correction and that you benefit therefrom. You shall not be required to utter The Act of Contrition or anything else to which you conscientiously object.

Certain other Correctional procedures, if needed, will be modified to allow for your inability to speak to God.

The Confessor

I am a retired lecturer. I have four science degrees including a doctorate. I have been happily married for forty-five years to a Catholic, the only woman I have ever known of the flesh. For the avoidance of doubt, and with great respect for my patient reader, I have never lain with a male person, nor ever desired him.

I am a Christian. As of 28 March 2025 I have been a Christian for twenty-eight years. For forty-five years I was an atheist.

I believe that redemption is achieved through suffering, for that is my experience. I believe that redemption through suffering is the Promise of The Teaching of Christ, epitomised forever by The Legacy of the Cross. It is not by chance that the symbol of my faith, uniquely, is a torture instrument. It is an unfashionable perspective, but not a cheerless one.

I consider that there are many paths to The Foot of the Cross. Non-Christian faiths and even atheism are utterly consistent with our search for spiritual perfection. A man or woman can be an excellent person, and improve to be a better one. They can do so living and dying in ignorance of Our Holy Savior, for they have all eternity in which to learn.

For some years I worshiped with The Society of Friends and contributed to their publications and charitable works. Over time, I gradually came to realise that I was unworthy of them, and I withdrew. In particular, a significant number of Britain Yearly Meeting were absolute pacifists and took active measures against the defence of my country. Theirs was neither treachery nor cowardice: On the contrary it was very brave and noble of them, done with an open hand and submission to the vengeance of the State. But I thought the policy and the practice ill-advised. Clearly, I consider that there is a place for violence in society. Rightly or wrongly, I think that there are circumstances in which violence, even lethal violence, conduces to both the physical survival and the spiritual health of *all* antagonists. It is another of life's paradoxes. It is no use mortal men and women trying to understand it.

When surgeons and others who may have to dispose of my remains ask I tell them I am a Christian and a Quaker.

I am a lifelong opponent of capital punishment and non-consensual corporal punishment. The spanking of children is unfair and unwise. It often produces lifelong and highly unedifying suffering for both guardian and child.

<u>My Promises to You</u>

I shall respect and treat you with tender kindness at all times. I shall never scorn or make light of anything you say or write. I shall never use harsh words or bad language. I shall pray for you, and for your Forgiveness from God. Where it is in my power I shall encourage your acquaintance to remit any anger or animosity towards you, and to forgive you in their hearts for any distress you have caused them, and to communicate their forgiveness and friendship to you.

I cannot make you do or say anything against your Faith or conscience, neither shall I attempt to do so.

I shall bring you closer to perfection through suffering and through joy.

I shall pay regard to your safety at all times and issue clear and simple instructions, and require your compliance. I shall hold you firmly through any ordeal but with minimum force. I shall pay due regard to your personal needs and follow any instruction of your medical advisors. I shall facilitate your prayer, your refreshment, and any reasonable cathartic act.

I shall maintain simple records of your identity and contact details as well as your birth date, sex, and special needs, as well as any details of consultations agreed with you. You may have a print-out of these records about you and you may order their alteration or deletion, which shall be executed. No third party shall access or peruse this data.

Our every call or meeting is a Holy Confessional Sacrament. I shall not divulge the fact or content of our meetings to any person whomsoever, unless you ask me to do so.

I shall never seek or suggest payment for anything.

<u>Your Rights and Duties</u>

Men and women have died hideously that you and I may confess our sins to God and worship Him in ways fitted to our understanding.

Article 18 of The United Nations Universal Declaration of Human Rights 1948 states:-

"Everyone has the right to freedom of thought, conscience and religion; this right includes the right to change his religion or belief and freedom, either alone, or in community with others, and in public or in private, to manifest his religion or belief in teaching, practice, worship and observance."

Yours rights include: The right to speak freely; freely to choose and marry your life partner and beget her children (or if you are a woman to bear his children); to travel; to work; to seek and take succour of medical aid if needful; to educate your children; to publish; to take your portion of the fruits of the earth; to assist others; to be equal under law; to participate in the councils of your nation and community to the best of your judgment and probity.

You have no right to God. Rather it is your solemn duty, if you are able, to love without hate, to honor the living and the dead, to reverence the world and its creatures, to prepare for your Perfection purchased by Someone Else, and to take the narrow but very rocky path He promised.

You may demand your rights. You can only await your Call.

The Mission of the Confessor

The Confessor takes a lonely road. He can gain no earthly recompense. His only wage will be the contumely of his neighbors and his persecution by the State. But such were ever the earnings of the true Christian.

He or she is the Sacrifice, in the company of his Penitents, his brothers and sisters in the collective Covenant.

The Confessor may get a thank-you from the more considerate of his brethren, or the occasional bottle of red wine, though even that shall of course be shared.

If he is a working man or woman, he will find it difficult to sustain a Sanctuary, unless, perhaps, he has a spare granny flat. He needs at least a bedroom with an adjacent bathroom. Hotels are hardly practicable, even in the daytime, and are exorbitantly expensive. The family home is equally impracticable, though I know that neighboring Sikhs here in Mercia maintain domestic shrine rooms.

All expense is the Confessor's to bear.

But enough of these gloomy and profitless thoughts.

A Confessor must be prospective and accentuate the positive at all times. His vocation is to make the world a better place, by humbly helping his penitents to be better people.

A Confessor cannot criticise those who canvass his ear, except in the most anodyne terms, much less of course can he betray them to the State or even an unsuspecting spouse.

If a male person is to confess a serious crime it will of course help to confess to a pastoress, unless he is remarkably happy to confide in another man.

Suppose a penitent arrives and says: "This morning I stole £8000 from a building society, I squirted ammonia at the teller, and shot two people as I left, one of whom is dead." The poor confessor is tempted to run, and to call the police. But she can only reply at worst: "You have been a very bad man, but we must look to the future, and do the right thing then. Please remove your clothing, Sir, and lie across my lap as we pray."

It is easy to be romantic about religion, and even easier to be romantic about people. But this is a Fallen world and we must be practical.

The murderer is not a coward: If he were he would not have entrusted his fate to the integrity of a pastoress. Therefore, once his anger and adrenaline have subsided it is likely that the logic of his predicament will compel him to seek the sanction of society. He may or may not ask for his Confessor's continuing assistance.

During Restoration it may be possible for the Confessor to broach the subject of the criminal handing himself in to the civil authorities; surrendering the money; and apologising to his victims or their survivors: Remember this latter is what Nedeljko did. This is the way to cleanse the culprit's spirit, knowing that he will lose everything else: The respect of others, his property (if any), his liberty, in some places his life. It is important to record the time of arrival of any penitent, and his time of departure. If the criminal faces a court of law you can, with the penitent's permission only, write to his counsel pointing-out that the prisoner attended Holy Correction and promised never to offend again. Of course you cannot go into detail, accept for any particulars that the Penitent agrees to disclose. Sometimes a judge will accept remorse in mitigation of punishment.

Or suppose a female arrives, we shall call her Jane, and she states "My boss, Mary, came to me and said I had wired 5.2 percent of our widgets defectively. The control threshold is five percent. I called her a stupid fat pig. She spent the rest of the morning crying in the lavatory. HR have given me a written warning."

What are you going to do with Jane?

You are going to say something like: "Oh, poor Jane: But more so poor Mary. Let's pray for her, and later maybe help God to make her happy again. Please undress, Jane, not forgetting your jewellery, and I will sit on the couch. You will lie across my thighs, tummy down."

During restoration you can ease whatever residual anger and resentment remains in Jane (very little if you have done your job properly) and explore tactful ways in which Jane might apologise to Mary. You might help Jane compose and write for herself a dignified but contrite apology, perhaps to accompany a flower delivery, but not a box of chocolates! A practical by-product may be the withdrawal of the warning, depending upon the wider state of morale in Mary's firm.

The only important thing to you is the spiritual welfare of your god-gifted Penitent. You must be callous to all other moral claims, the feelings of the victims, the retribution of the State, your own convenience, your umbrage at the crime.

It is not easy. You would prefer a sound spanking yourself, all day, and every day of the week.

To those who say that the Confessor has betrayed his country and his community I say this: Which is best for the long term progress of the people, a kind and respectful but memorably painful correction lasting an hour or two; or thirty-year prison sentences, dismissals or indeed executions involving thousands and terrorising millions?

<u>Real Penitents</u>

Among several tactics that may be deployed to discriminate genuine penitents from timewasters the following is possibly the most easy and failsafe. Ask the prospective penitent to replace his clothing (if he is already undressed) and ask him to clean and tidy the Sanctuary. The genuine penitent will obey you instantly. If he or she seeks requisites, provide them to hand. Order any shoddy work to be re-done. After you are satisfied with his work in the Sanctuary tell him to strip and clean the lavatory and the bathroom. Interrupt him for prayers, and tell him to pray aloud for his victim, and then for you the Confessor. Then tell him to resume work in the wet rooms. After a minute or two stop his efforts and tell him to use the lavatory and take a shower. Bring him a glass of cool drinking water. If the subject is male, as tactfully as you can, invite him to have a spanked Correction if he wishes it. If the subject is female lead her gently to the couch and invite her to assume the position. If the female shakes her head or makes any other expression of reluctance then interpret the signal as non-consent to spanking. *Do not oblige a female to request physical contact.* In any case, make it clear they can continue their non-contact penances if they prefer such.

The genuine Penitent will not take umbrage at the implied insult of your doubt. Rather he will accept it as a natural part of his mortification.

If the penitent responds in the negative to invitation offer him or her a seat (not necessarily at your side, unless they wish it) and move directly to Restoration routines, perhaps with bread and wine, or even a cup of tea or coffee. They may remain naked unless it is clear that the state distresses them.

If the putative penitent demurs at any juncture, courteously request that he leaves the Sanctuary but that when he is psychologically and spiritually prepared for Penance he is most welcome to return.

Remember, you have already engaged a Holy Sacrament with your first order to the prospective penitent. Never a raised voice, never any sign or signal of impatience. No lectures. No sermons. You are always kind, always compassionate. Always ready to believe the best, but sedulous to test trust. You trust and verify. Except for necessary commands and advice, you always bestow the gift of silent penances interrupted only by the penitent's prayers, or your prayer for him. Always your utmost to heal and repair, and when the time is right, to listen. Always your utmost to honor God.

I have made the tests of *bona fides* seem very stereotyped and programmatic. As you know, Holy Correction should be flexible and varied, full of surprise and delight. You are of course welcome to vary the tasks you impose *ad libitum*, regarding only the safety and dignity of your actual or prospective penitent. After a spanked Reparation you would think nothing of congratulating your Penitent with some little token of esteem: Perhaps a flower, a box of chocolates, a prayer pamphlet, one of those cheap metal crucifixes Catholics deposit at wayside shrines, maybe all four and a treble. The key to understanding the eclipse of the big vanilla denominations is the arid routine of their rituals, and in particular the pattered, perfunctory prayer of their purported confessions.

The Expression of Emotion

Spanking can often though unpredictably excite, besides resistance, the expression of strong passive emotion. Such passive expression can include laughter, weeping or sexual arousal, or even all three in a quasi-simultaneous outburst.

Hand spanking is not, of itself, sufficiently painful to reduce a healthy adult to tears. Any crying excited is mostly due to psycho-spiritual factors: Shame, remorse, resentment, humiliation, anger or any combination of such emotions.

The fact has to be faced that hand-spanking is both erotic and highly emotive and its psychic efficacy may hinge upon both those aspects.

The keys to a Confessor's successful negotiation of phases of crisis are calmness, kindness, prayer and time. I emphasise that a Correction should never be hurried. It is not a race against the clock. Even if your Penitent dies during the course of his Sacrament, he dies in a better and happier condition than he entered it, whatever the agents of the State may say. You should smile kindly and reassure, avoiding any apparent insincerity, and be generous with kisses, cuddles and praise.

Correctional spanking is of its nature Safe, Sane and Consensual: Accordingly, any resistance other than a transitory reflex is obviously a cause for cancellation or postponement of the spanking element of the Sacrament though the Confessional itself may continue with alternative Penances if your subject and yourself agree to such.

Laughter, weeping and arousal distract the Penitent from prayer and study partially negating the purpose of his presentation and impeding his route to ecstasy.

All three are crises that must be handled with great skill and tact by the Confessor, taxing all his patience but clearing the ground for great rewards. The situation is complicated by the fact that in working-class and middle-class British culture most participants have hang-ups surrounding weeping and arousal in particular. Your (opposite sex) penitent may have rejected sex play or full Union as a remedy outright, and Anglo males are likely to think themselves more than remiss if they shed a single tear.

In Anglo culture, stoicism or the affectation of stoicism can be a passive resistance in its own right. Stoicism can also impede progress and spoil your subject's enjoyment of his Correction. But accept it with calmness, restraint and prayerful courtesy. It is probably meant as a courtesy to you.

In a sense, laughter is the least of your problems. It is likely to disappear once the subject settles down. The entire Correction should be a joyous event, notwithstanding the physical pain, and laughter is much to be preferred to tears. It definitely does not infer that your Penitent is failing to take his correction seriously: Believe me, he is going to remember his spanking anyway, just make sure he remembers it for the right reasons. The real misery, and the real release from pain, should be within his Soul. There is nothing wrong with responding to, or even encouraging laughter, with a well-timed jest or pleasantry, but that will test your skills even further. After all, you are a confessor, not a comedian.

I will say little of sexual arousal. If your strikes are rapid and distinctly painful, arousal may well be avoided altogether. A reasonable way of propelling your Penitent into a correct frame of mind is to start with ten rapid blows, five on the lower part of each buttock, above the gluteal fold. This may well be all that is needed. Or all that is *ever* necessary.

Though weeping impedes intellectual aspects of the Sacrament it is of great physiological benefit to the Penitent, improving hormonal tone and (correctly managed) oxygenation, assisting the eventual spiritual benefits of the total experience, especially for women. There is no point in over-spanking the determined stoic. We are not here to "teach a lesson" or to "beat the evil out of" someone. But having said that, if the subject starts to mewl or whimper do him the favor of a few more firm and rapid blows in the hope of fluid crying. Once that starts, lead him through a few (maybe three) deep and slow breaths, patiently allowing for his obvious lack of respiratory control. Always kindness, always quiet authority, always "take your time, Honey."

If you have read this far I do not think I really need to write that you should never attempt nasty tricks from the literature. We are not torturers. In particular, never strike any part of the leg or foot with a wand. It will bring tears for sure, but at the expense of damage to the vascular tissue or the sciatic nerve, or likely both.

You are entitled to use humane methods to encourage weeping if you consider your Penitent is going to benefit from the experience. If he seems to be attempting an obdurate stoicism onerous *for him* then you can resort to a measure only to be used in this crisis: The *very softest reproach*. Tell your penitent explicitly that he is a brave and lovely person and you cannot understand why he committed his crime, whatever it was. Tell him that his very attendance proves his virtue, but his crime was very wicked (even if you consider it somewhat ridiculous), and that his poor victim must be feeling very miserable. If truly necessary, voice a forensic dissection of his offense, elaborating its consequences and ramifications, especially for those he never intended to injure. Tell him that God wants him to be a building, loving person who will pray for the solace of his victim and later take positive measures to afford restitution to his victim, and expiation of his own crime before God. Cite the passages of Scripture (in his religion) relative to his sin. Whilst you are giving this verbal encouragement hold the Penitent's far buttock firmly but supportively, and give it a gentle squeeze at points you wish to emphasise. Make the subject feel secure, loved, forgiven and quite ashamed. If he is going to cry he will start now. Then allow him a few moments of prayerful silence. Next, rehearse aloud the Confessor's Prayer of Thanksgiving for Tears, and then softly lead the Penitent through the reciprocal equivalent, reminding him to take his time. Give him a kiss and a cuddle. Then maybe a phase of massage and hydration before further devotions. Use a non-allergenic paper tissue to wipe away his tears and blow his nose for him.

Do not permit yourself to be distracted or deterred by thoughts of abomination, or, heaven forfend, accuse yourself of such. Clearly, it helps if you are of opposite sex to your Penitent. But you do not have to be. If the intimacy is giving you problems, stay fully clothed.

Humility

The key to making your Correction a success is deep humility, not just on your part but also on mine, the Confessor. We have got to put our natural human vanities and prejudices aside for a few hours. I have got to find the patience to listen and learn from you, to understand your problems and your situation. I have to do something very difficult for me: Refrain from value judgment. I must resist the temptation, as far as I am able, to tell you what an awful person you are, knowing that compared to me you must be a paragon of virtue. I have got to try to understand what it is you need, and what God needs from you. For a distinctly unpleasant minute or two I have then to hit you without stint but also without spite.

For your part, as a Penitent, you have to admit that you have harmed, physically or psychically, some other person or animal. You have to admit that you did this unjustly, and that you must suffer for your sin in this life. If you are a believer you must further concede that but for God's Grace, you will suffer in the next. You must admit that compensation is impossible but that you will search for practical ways to ameliorate your crime and improve your future behaviour. Perhaps hardest of all, especially in view of your understandable nervousness, you must never offer any word of mitigation or self-exculpation.

You cannot benefit from your Holy Correction unless you submit absolutely to the will and hand of your Confessor for the duration of the meeting, without complaint and without criticism. Your questions and requests should be directed to eliciting understanding of your offence, and why it is against God's Law.

It is not easy.

Yet by one of those strange paradoxes of life though my mastery seems complete, it is actually you who can and may well extract a fountain of cleansing from a Correction away from which you stride victor.

At worst you have wasted a weekend afternoon painfully with a bore. At best you have had the loveliest and most fulfilling Communion with God you have ever had: Truly a life-changing event. Perhaps a transverberation.

It is your Correction. You make the most of it.

At the more mundane level, you must do or say nothing to increase my own feelings of pride or ascendancy. Never address me as Master, Sir, Reverence or anything else abnormal: Jim is perfectly appropriate. (Matthew 23:10). I will address you by your Christian name, or your familiar name in your community. I will make every effort to address you by name. But I may call you Honey, Darling, Beautiful or some other silly endearment during the meeting. This is likely irrespective of your age or sex. Believe me, I know how annoying this is, having endured it myself. Please do not complain during Correction. I will very gladly apologise if asked after the sacrament. If you call me something silly but not disrespectful I shall not admonish you.

Our Holy Savior promised that the meek shall inherit the Earth, and so they shall. As they did on that day long ago when tiny creatures peered furtively from their burrows to watch the thundering dinosaurs breathe their last. (Matthew 5:5).

Christ added: "But I say unto you, That ye resist not evil: but whoever shall smite thee on thy right cheek, turn to him the other also." (Matthew 5:39).

For it is the very nature of prophesy that it is foretold in the figure and fulfilled in the letter.

Humility is the sovereign antidote to the king and progenitor of all Sins: Pride.

Walk with humility and walk with God.

Man: You are not a sap or a weakling because you literally lie down and take a beating. On the contrary, you show the capacity to spurn aside hardship and insult as you stride decisively to your strategic objective. Humility is strength.

Woman: Do not be ashamed if a man beholds your portal of life. It is a holy thing. Such a sight was our first on Earth, and the man truly offended of it has not been born. Humility is purity.

<u>Organisational Outline</u>

Correction begins with your first statement of sin, your sacrosanct Confession, accepted at face value, and followed by voiced and silent prayers.

A Reparation penance phase will involve a number of painful blows delivered with the flat of the hand to your bottom. No instrument is ever used. It is impossible for me to be specific about the number or strength of the strikes or to make more than a very vague attempt to be commensurate. That being understood, I shall try to adjust the penance to the seriousness of the offence and your personal condition at the time, but you will always suffer what is needful and complete. We shall not converse during Reparation. I may give orders to be obeyed. Please do not count the blows. In longer Reparations much of the time will be given over to prayer, recuperation and exercise.

The second Restoration phase will commence with a prayer that I shall say aloud offering your pain as Reparation for your sin, beseeching no further penalty on Earth or in The Life to Come. You may continue your prayers, quietly meditate, or discuss with me anything you wish. Please avoid, however, larger issues beyond immediate relevancy. You may want to talk over plans for practical reparations to those you have sinned against. After that, I will give priority to saying the prayers or readings that you have requested. I will then look for a relevant passage of Scripture for you to read or have read, if you are thus consoled. We may have a comfort break, some coffee, or at appropriate times a simple meal, if needed.

No animal need die to feed us in our Sanctuary. We are apes, frugivores, and abide as the herbivores God planned. We shall seek no Sacrifice. We are it.

At some juncture in either phase we will have a little bread to eat and a sip of red wine each *taken in silence and without comment* by either party. If you are strictly abstinent then we shall both have blackcurrant juice or tomato juice instead of wine. If you are allergic or intolerant to certain foods please let me know by email or letter well in advance of presentation.

This two-stage cycle can be repeated for each sin you wish to confess, or consolidated at your will.

I make your Correction sound very structured and regimented but there is of course room for flexibility without in any way spoiling your experience.

At the end of the whole Correction session you are Blessed.

<u>Behaviour</u>

If under stress, you scream, plead, swear or otherwise show that you have not prepared to have your Confession heard at this time then I may terminate the meeting forthwith. Minor insanctities will be admonished but overcome. Neither sexual arousal nor heartfelt crying are insanctity, and do not necessarily disrupt your Correction. If I perceive that such conditions are developing I may take measures to get you through and over any crisis so that you can re-focus your thoughts on spiritual matters.

Minor insanctities include things like chattering, gossiping (this may implicate more serious sin), answering back, or making trivial requests. I will try to keep a sense of humor but, unless we know one another really well, I cannot simply pat you on the bottom and call you a naughty girl (or boy): That is striking in spite. I will give you a gentle touch or some other felt reminder to keep quiet. Your penance is for your pain and your prayers. During a Reparation I will not speak myself unless for safety, or I am moved to prayer for you, or you ask me to say a prayer with you.

Gross insanctities include, by example: Denying the Merit of God or that of a prophet of any faith; Proselytising; Commending or deprecating any party political policy or any policy of state; Simulation or affectation of any emotion or intellectual position. Gross insanctity is always a wilful choice: It is impossible to commit a gross insanctity by accident. I may abort a sacrament defiled by a gross insanctity. Please use your safe word if you must terminate instantly.

I am unable to punish insanctities, or indeed anything else. Reverent expression of doubt about anything is not an insanctity. I shall assume that any voiced prayer is sincere, even, or perhaps especially, if uttered by a professed atheist.

Resistance, or, as observed elsewhere, sexual arousal or weeping are not insanctities, though such behaviours may delay or disrupt your Holy Correction. These or other crises may require your Correction to be suspended or postponed until you are able to continue, though the Sacrament shall remain current until your Blessing at its conclusion. At best, the delay may only be a few minutes.

<u>Reverential Respect</u>

From the moment we meet I shall respect you. People who admit they are wrong are a rare breed. People who admit they are wrong and wicked are a tiny subset of that rare breed. People who admit they are wrong and wicked but have the will to change are an infinitesimal subset of a subset of a subset.

People who admit they are wrong and wicked and need a hiding and willingly of free choice will take one are an elite. Of such are saints and martyrs made. Of such unknown heroes and immortal fame and the undying obscurity of country fanes.

As our fellowship ages and deepens my respect for you will grow.

By the time I cross you and kiss you I shall have special feelings for you. Elsewhere I call that feeling veneration but it is the wrong word. It is too weak a word. If I could choose the word to express my thought then, by definition, this would not be existential experience and I would not have followed Kierkegaard and the rest into the inexpressible, the infinite abyss of the indescribable, the unknowing.

Even Our Holy Savior did not attempt the ineffable but rather drew by allegory, told literal Truths in the figure, and demonstrated Good Works. He asked that the cup be taken from Him in the garden, but he was neither wrong nor wicked and of free choice took a Hiding.

This is not of either love or liking: It is a trajection along some indeliniable extra dimension of acclaim.

By the time you have rested under my hand I shall know that not only are you wise and modest, but that you are also very, very brave.

When you obey me it is an act of love beyond mere trust. You know, or think you know, that to comply will bring a reward of acute pain and imminent psychic danger. To obey and of free choice to obey is an act of heroism on a couch, and savors more of conquest than surrender. For though your obedience honors me, it transfigures you.

You owe me nothing. You do not need to thank me at any time. Indeed you need say nothing but your confessions and your prayers during our entire meeting. But if you make even a hint of approval I shall be overcome with gratitude, and if you thank me after your Blessing I shall certainly cry.

Make The Sign of The Cross by all means. I sometimes do. But no precaution is necessary, whether of a sacred or a profane kind. Spanking, accurately administered and calmly borne, is safer than a dental filling made with local anaesthetic.

I shall do what I can to arrange for the golden glow of sunlight to slant across your body for at least part of our meeting. But Britain is of course a cloudy country, and in an English winter, and even more a Scottish, the Sun skims shyly across the horizon and takes an early bath. If the light causes you the least discomfort I shall shade it.

Experienced penitents are confident and happy, pleased to confess and to worship. They can read the Sun and the stars and the signs of spiritual shoals ahead. They can kedge through such shallows or steer off with flawless skill.

If you are female: Please do not curtsy or render any other gesture of deference, and certainly not when naked. Neither do you need to smile if you do not wish to. I know that you might do these things for my sake, to ease my anxiety, but believe me, in the circumstances, and in my likely condition, such will do me no favor. A pillow will lie between us, but if you detect tumidity please do not take offence. I am a man and have a man's involuntary reflexes. Know that my reverence for you is absolute.

If you are male: I will expect, and very probably get, no deference. This is as it should be. I will try to be efficient, but be assured that I shall be neither summary nor perfunctory. You will have all the time and all the kindly regard that you need. If you weep it is not a problem. Real men do not hesitate to express tender emotion.

<u>How does this Work?</u>

Confessional Spanking Therapy (CST) has both physiological and spiritual aspects. We would like to dispense with the former and embrace the latter in Perfection, but we are Fallen creatures and in this life congress with the Divine is mediated through our bodies.

I shall certainly not suggest that we approach God by tripping-off on drugs, whether the drugs arise from within our bodies or enter from outwith. But what I need to clarify is that the total process generates biochemical secretions that modify both our behaviour in and appreciation of Holy Correction. To know this is to have the power to make the most of God's Gifts.

At different stages organs in the brain and the chest will secrete various hormones or animal opiates that will condition your mood in different ways.

Initially, and especially if you are a novice, your natural apprehensiveness will cause your adrenal gland to secrete the defence hormone adrenaline. I too will experience this to some extent. This will engender an unpleasant, keyed-up feeling of vague dread. The hormone cortisol may also reflect your stress.

As soon as we start, adrenaline levels will drop suddenly, your heart rate will slow, and you will begin to relax. Because at some subconscious animal level, spanking is a dominance-submission social behaviour, you will soon begin to feel the effects of oxytocin. This is a polypeptide reproductive hormone that is made in the hypothalamus and that seeps from the pituitary gland embedded in your brain. Oxytocin is produced by both males and females. In women it assists childbirth contractions and lactation. Oxytocin can reduce acute pain by up to thirty percent, and drastically more in those chronically stressed. From our viewpoint, the psychological effects of this chemical are more important. Oxytocin is not prurient or aphrodisiac but it produces a whole-body sexual response in both sexes. You feel desperately submissive and sympathetic, as if you wish to immerse yourself in the care and nurturing of a child or some other loved object. It feels very spiritual but is not wholly so. Certainly you feel vaguely in love and at peace with the world. You will want to pray and possibly to cry. Once your pituitary stops seeping oxytocin into the bloodstream you will recover from its effects within ten minutes. Having said that, the pituitary may continue to lace your blood with oxytocin for weeks after your penance!

Because oxytocin induces childbirth, for that reason and the obvious mechanical hazards, I cannot confess a woman in advanced pregnancy.

By a later, third, stage the acute pain of your spanking will have prompted your body to secrete endorphins into the bloodstream. Endorphins are animal narcotics chemically similar to the vegetable alkaloids nicotine, morphine and hyoscine. Their physiological effect is very similar. The endorphins sooth the pain from your nerve endings, and induce a dreamy, peaceful and invulnerable sensation. You may continue to feel emotional, but arousal will not be a problem, and you will feel ready more steadily to commune with God and consider the spiritual aspects of your past and future.

At the end of a fully-successful Correction you will be in a state of transcendental trance and physically exhausted. You may fall asleep, and would be allowed to sleep indefinitely.

<u>Preparation for Correction</u>

Formulate in your mind a list of sins that you wish to confess. Try not to anticipate the physical consequences. When the time comes I shall give you what you need, not what you want, or what suits my convenience. Remember the words of

Jesus, "𝔖ufficient unto the day is the evil thereof" (Matthew 6:34). It may help to write your sins on paper, and bring it with you. Be brief and stick to the who, the where and the how. Lengthy disquisitions are not needed and encourage excuses!

Please do not take alcohol or psychotropic drugs, including prescription drugs, before your Correction. If prescription medications are essential please check with your advisors that they are compatible with cardiovascular stress, and inform the Confessor of your medical needs and precautions.

I will provide you with cold still or sparkling water in an unbreakable cup, and set it where you can reach it. You can have as much water, or indeed any other reasonable refreshment, as you need.

If you wish to bring a friend (for support) weigh carefully her feelings. This is a violent event and very unsettling for onlookers. It is a good idea to arrange a time and date convenient for her before arranging a meeting with me.

Travel to Correction in comfortable, casual clothing. There is no need for elegance or formality.

Please do not wear make-up or piercings.

Do not wear jewellery beyond a secure wedding band. Remove especially studs and earrings and anything that is around, or can slip onto, the neck. Wear no bandana or hair-fastener. Remove your wristwatch and all bangles. If you wear glasses I shall remove them during your Reparations. I will remove any loose or hazardous items I find, and in the case of any apparently religious apparel I shall pass it into your hand.

Please turn off mobiles and other electronic alarms. Please do not bring devotional materials upon electronic devices, unless required for your disabilities or special needs.

Bring a Holy Bible or the Holy Scripture of your faith, prayers, or other spiritually-significant literature that you wish to read or discuss, or have me read to you. Additionally, you may bring a religious object or cuddly toy to hold as you serve penance. Make sure that the object is safe if wrung. A Holy Bible will always be available to you.

<u>Bringing a Friend</u>

You may wish to bring someone along. Be wise and kind, and consider their feelings very carefully, even before you invite them.

Any third person in your Correction will suffer much more grievously than you, even a professional advisor or indeed a stranger.

I will not resent your companion, but their welcome will be my admonition that they must never refer to or hint at anything they are about to witness for the rest of their lives. If they do not agree, or do not seem to be taking the matter seriously, I will show them the door.

Your companion will get zero moral support or consolation from me. All my spiritual and social attention will be focused upon you. I shall not so much as ask him or her if he wants a cup of coffee, though of course he will get one if we have one ourselves.

A female acquaintance from your church or club might prove ideal. She might well caress and console you through the bleakest moments without excessive emotion or disruptiveness. Remember that when the pain is sharpest I must keep silence. In Quakerdom they are all ministers of God, but an actual priestess of another denomination may have to seek the sanction of her superiors.

You will know your own circumstances much better than I but in general terms it is unwise to involve a male friend. They are easily aroused and few have the personal humility or the steady nerve demanded. Also males are reluctant to touch either sex. If you are female a man's natural instincts are to protect you and also to prevent contact with a second adult male. Are you able to conceive the thoughts of a husband or father presented with the sights and sounds we shall raise? It would be better if they confessed you themselves.

Giving Up to Grow Stronger

Penance and confession are about the surrender of sin. That evil is lodged firmly in your heart and mind, and it is impossible to remove unless you submit unconditionally. Even your Reparations will not be a monotonous tribulation of beating. You are not being punished. There will be plenty of time to relax, and for quiet prayer and reflection. Just give up. Let your Confessor do with you what he or she will. She or he will do nothing evil, but even if they do their sin is not yours, for you did not consent. You were silent. Your Confessor has a mutual interest in success. He or she will do just enough to make you contrite, and no more. Remember, it might be his turn next!

The Evil in your heart is not yours. It belongs to Satan. It is not his fault. You stole it. It is time to turn it in to the competent Authorities. They will return it to its rightful Owner.

Holy Correction is about empowering your spirit and impelling you into the frame of mind in which you hate your sin and reject it with loathing. God intervenes because he is on your side. He has heard your prayers and knows what you want. In our dreadful modern jargon your Confessor is a mere facilitator. When you have the power you can step forward in strength, re-enter your normal environment and put your life right. You are, as it were, a new man or a new woman, a better person, and you act like one.

Holy Correction is a therapy. Sorry about the clinical language but you are a living animal and a dynamic physicochemical system. Your Confessor is looking for every subtle change in your mood and tone actively to optimise your path to moral cleansing. He or she is on your side. He will get you where you want to be as quickly as possible, but without rushing you, and with minimum fuss. He will give you a few hard spanks to set you on your way, a rub, maybe a massage, another set of slaps, or a wipe. This is why I cannot publish a tariff, and one of several good reasons why I ask you not to count. You are an individual. This is for you personally.

Your Confessor will say a few spoken prayers for you to share and not a few highly unprofessional words of encouragement! He or she has a lonely job to do. So he will be really glad if you ask him to say one of your prayers with you, a few words at a time please, so he can get it right. Please forgive him if he garbles a sacred text in your language. At some time during a Reparation your confessor will ask you to say aloud a prayer known as The Act of Contrition. This is not an oath. It is your pledge to God that you want to renounce your sin and you want Him to help you do so. If you find this difficult to remember, your confessor will help by prompting you a few words at a time. Short of sexual assault your Confessor may do anything safe with your body. Your mind remains yours and your soul was always God's property. When you are used to the blows and will not writhe into danger your Confessor will not restrain you so tightly. He may just rest his spare hand on your head or the small of your back. He will rest his spanking hand on your thigh: Your bottom will soon be hot and sore. Usually he will tacitly warn you of incoming strikes, perhaps with a very gentle tap or squeeze. But Correction should be full of surprises, some of them delightful! The postures are awkward for both the Penitent and his Confessor. You will need to be lifted or shifted, and your Confessor may need to straddle you and give you a massage. These practical activities prevent bad circulation, the formation of blood clots, and muscle cramps. They also soothe unnecessary or distracting pains. An old or weak Confessor will need your active assistance. They will speak very kindly, but mean to be taken seriously. Obey him or her instantly without quibble. You do not have to say anything, not even Yes or Thank You.

It will seem that your Holy Confessor is treating your body with an outrageous and childish insolence. Well, maybe, maybe not. Believe me, he or she is looking down upon you in complete awe. His respect for you is total. Indescribable.

With skill, tact and forbearance on both sides this potentially revolting experience can be fashioned into an ecstasy of a stately and tender beauty, almost as sacred as that most sacred thing you thought about. Something that sets you up not just for the day, but for the month, or, at best, for a lifetime.

Our Meeting

When you arrive you will be greeted by me and offered coffee or a comfort break. I shall not bore you with any tedious, self-regarding lectures. It is God you have offended, not me. You will briefly be reminded that each sin you have declared, or shall later confess, will be responded to in two phases:-

Reparation and Restoration as previously described.

When you are ready you may offer your next sin for redress, unless you have consolidated.

Leave sore but happy. If there are tears, I sincerely hope you also have laughter!

At some time during your penance, I will request you to voice The Act of Contrition and give you any required help with it. The timing of this will depend upon your progress. The Act is your rejection of the sin confessed and you have the right and duty to refuse it until you are ready.

If during the Correctional meeting you appear to be trying to pray I shall pause what I am doing, especially if it is painful, to give you time to collect your thoughts. You can take it from me, this also applies to professed atheists!

If during a Reparation you need to shift your position or visit the lavatory say "Pause." Do so only in emergency. If I am doing my job I will already have perceived your need.

Before the meeting we will have agreed a safeword that you can use to gain immediate disengagement. In any case, no artificial restraint is used and, whilst you are held safely, you can roll clear of blows at any time. That does not necessarily cancel our meeting and if you wish, and we are physically and mentally up to it, we may restart as if the interruption never happened.

You naturally would like a forecast of the number and severity of the blows you will endure, but as I remark elsewhere I am unable to predict that. In general, I will try to avoid hitting so hard that bruising persists, or so softly that arousal or even boredom become problems. I will try to err on the side of fewer and heavier. I do not intend to waste your time. You need to Confess to God.

If the Worst Happens

Correctional Spanking Therapy of any kind is not for everyone.

If it is not for you the fact will usually have emerged in prior interviews or correspondence. But in the context of Holy Correction the first five minutes of penance is often the make or break time. Very tenacious individuals may make it to the end of a Correction, but nevertheless leave offended.

Maybe you need a gentler form of sacrament or maybe just a talk with a friend.

It is natural, especially if you are new, to experience feelings of anger and affront when you are hit. If distress or agitation appears I shall pause briefly and pray aloud, asking God to take from you your anger and shame, to annihilate these evils, and to restore to you a calm mind and a clean soul. We may do a breathing exercise together, if it helps you. Occasionally, a psychosomatic body trembling may arise. If so I shall postpone further spanking indefinitely and wrap you in the duvet to prevent chill. I shall take you in my arms and say the Prayer. Any resistance will be softly admonished. Then I will tell you explicitly that the blows are an assault upon your body not an insult to your honor. On the contrary, that the pain is your Sacred Earnest of your desire for reform, a personal pledge of honor, and that the strikes are a mark of my high esteem for you. If you begin to cry that is a good sign, but a quite separate crisis which we will deal with in a different way.

Of course you may utter your safeword at any time. The result will be that I cease immediately whatever I am doing and release you. The sacrament will terminate and you will be unshriven of the sin. But I will continue to treat you with the civility and kindness of ordinary friendship. As you dress you will be offered coffee or perhaps a stiff drink, if you are not driving. If you wish it, I will be happy to talk about our problems or the issues that arose. Obviously, you can have an analgesic.

Think of your safeword as if the ejector seat in an aircraft. Its deployment is traumatic of itself, and an act of desperation perpetrated to evade an imminent and much greater disaster. You should not of course request anything during a penance but it is preferable that you ask, as reverentially as possible, for clemency. Clemency does not void the sacrament.

Please remember that I can never apologise for a prayer or an inflicted penance or any other act committed with sacred intent. Neither of course can I apologise for the totality of the Holy Correction itself, even if it suffers abortion at outset.

What I can and will say sorry for is any ineptitude, error or rudeness I have perpetrated, and I will beg you to forgive me.

In very sad situations other things can happen.

Always bear in mind that I cannot spank you for minor insanctities or even major ones. I cannot punish. I can only give you the pain you need for your own purpose. Also, recursive shriving is impossible. That is I cannot take a confession of a sin that you actually committed in this Correction. It must wait for a separate meeting, if at all.

If you protest that you do not deserve what you are getting I shall explicitly ask you this question: Did Jesus deserve to be scourged? I shall await your reply. If you fail to reply, or your reply fails to satisfy me, I shall abort the sacrament on the grounds of gross insanctity. One truthful answer exists, and if you give it I shall ask that we continue your Holy Correction normally.

If you claim that you cannot tolerate more pain I shall ask you if you wish to make a formal plea for clemency. If you refuse we will continue. If you want clemency I shall ask you to kneel on the floor facing me, to clasp your hands prayerfully, look into my eyes, and then close yours. This is not ritual humiliation. This is Correctional penance.

You will then pray to God, not of course myself.

I should not want my Penitent to attempt flattery or manipulation. The former would be bad for my soul, and the latter even worse for the spirit of my charge. Rather my Penitent should pray to God in silence, asking the Most Merciful to intercede with the Confessor. After an interval I would ask you, the Penitent, if he had finished. If he answered affirmatively I would gently ask him to return to my lap.

If God guides me I will make a decision which may be to continue your Reparation normally. It is, however, unlikely that I shall continue to strike you. I may impose a different penance. A number of options are open to us. None are dishonorable. Special procedures apply to atheists or agnostics who wish to apply for clemency.

If there are no more blows, you and I shall share a prayer together to thank God for His mercy.

None of this is done to hurt you, to punish you, or because I want to take a nasty vengeance. Remember that today I am your Holy Confessor, and because of that I have an abiding care for you and a Sacred Trust that I cannot betray. And until I give you your valedictory Blessing I have actively to prosecute your spiritual management.

Therefore though we may have annoyed one another, I have to do what is best, under God's Guidance but within the scope of my personal limitations, for your Immortal Spirit. You have a right to break your Sacrament, and you can choose to do so reverently or profanely. It is your rightful right, won for you by others. I must fulfil my pledge of trust that you won and hold by showing me your body and your soul.

Of course, secular control rests in your hands at all times and you can demand the return of your human rights by exercising your safeword, or simply getting up and leaving.

It is possible to rescue a damaged sacrament and bring it to a distant but happy conclusion. That would require immense fortitude on your part, some degree of tact upon mine, and almost monastic standards of humility from each of us.

Also remember that however awful your reception was my door is always open to you. Once you have lain naked across my lap there is a special bond of trust between us. I may not be your idea of a friend but ours is a fellowship that no recrimination can defile, nor the years erase. I will always listen to your problems, and offer what advice I can, if God guides me.

<u>Your First Five Minutes</u>

Your first five minutes will be really tough but my heart and my prayers will be with you. If you are a novice it will be doubly stressful, and if you belong to the generations thankfully never spanked by a parent or a spouse trebly so.

I shall be as courteous and as sensitive as I am able. My almost overwhelming temptation will be to apologise after the first strike, and give you a rub and a hug. Remember, I cannot apologise for anything sacramental I do, though I can after the Blessing for technical errors. Indeed, I am very limited in anything I can say in the Reparation phase.

Even the bravest penitents will be nervous at this stage. I expect this and allow for it. You may be surprised to find that I am also nervous and expectant.

I know that you seldom if ever swear, and would certainly not wilfully do so in Holy Correction. Be aware that this sacrament involves sudden and painful mechanical shocks. Especially avoid, if you can, breaches of The Third Commandment, the injunction not to take the Lord's Name in vain. I reserve the right to terminate an abused Correction.

After our preliminaries I shall invite you to undress. If undressing before a man is an issue for you I shall leave the room and invite you to settle prone on our couch before you call me back in. Otherwise I shall sit on the couch and look down in prayer. Please be sure to remove every artificial thing except your wedding band and necessary medical or prosthetic appliances.

If I am sitting and you approach me I shall look up and into your eyes, stand, and take you by the hand.

I shall sit beneath you and place pillows beneath your head and your pelvis. I shall gently adjust your position.

I shall make sure that your hand items are placed by your pillow where you can reach them but before your first Reparation we will be especially careful for your safety. I will gently but firmly hold you.

I shall hear your first sin, even if you have already mentioned it or sent it in writing.

I shall ask you to read or recite a prayer for my purity, good management and good conduct throughout our meeting. If you wish to substitute that with a prayer of your own composition, or omit it altogether, you may do so without giving offence.

Then I shall pray aloud, according to my Christian faith, for your steadfastness, your entire spiritual satisfaction, the entire and irrevocable destruction of your sin, and your forgiveness from God and man.

Be aware that I am unable to invite you to tell me when to start, or to encourage you to solicit anything during a sacrament.

I shall ask you if you are comfortable, and if you answer in the affirmative I shall commence your penance briskly and strongly. It is only in exceptional cases of the most complete and manifest contrition that I shall forbear to strike.

During your Reparation I will do what is possible to persuade you to relax and accept whatever happens calmly. We will speak, however, as minimally as possible. Your response will depend utterly on your individual personality, your habits of mind, and your mood at the time. Some respond with equanimity, even flippancy. Other reactions do not reflect upon your courage or character: You have already proven both.

<u>Settling In</u>

If you begin to sob or whimper I will try to make you weep freely as soon as possible. This will improve your respiration, and further promote the release of stress-relieving body chemicals. All this will help allay your fear and bring nearer the onset of spiritual transcendence. I will also give you a cuddle, more in congratulation than consolation! And if you are a man, remember that there is nothing sissy about crying into a teddy bear if you are being beaten.

If I weep, be not dismayed. It is no reflection upon you or your conduct. It is an ordinary human response to suffering, to our storm of Witness, and to the overwhelming Love of God that shall be raining down upon and through us, like, so to speak, cosmic radiation.

After the first twenty minutes or half an hour our nervousness will go and we will become increasingly relaxed and cheerful. If you have been crying you will almost certainly have stopped, though tearfulness may later begin or resume as you apprehend the full horror of your past wickedness.

Ecstatic effects do not always supersede for everyone, and not at every Correction even for the experienced.

But if we are fully successful by The Grace of God, sometime toward the end of the first (or perhaps only) hour you will enter a mind state of transcendental sanctity. You will yearn for total submersion in worship and Divine communion. An almost childlike feeling of submission and acceptance will well through your entire frame and you will feel ready cheerfully to walk over hot coals hand-in-hand with God Himself. Not that you will get the opportunity to do so on my carpet!

For sure, some of this is due to hormone and endorphin inebriation, but the best is due to supernatural interventions to which even atheists are not immune. You may not believe in God, but God believes in you.

What You are Really Like

By the closing stages of your Correction I shall view you with great veneration. Your courage, honesty and piety will be very clear indeed. So too will be your meekness, your kindness and your temperance. Truly you will have succeeded in your Imitation of Christ, even if you think of that by another Name in your belief system. You will have noticed how reluctant I am to speak of love in these pages. I do not intend to abuse the word or the concept. But the emotion I feel shall approximate it.

I will make the effort to voice my admiration. If you have a trusted friend, I will already have asked him to fill in the details.

Blessing

I cannot grant Absolution: No mortal can for it is the prerogative of Christ alone. At the end of your Correction I shall apply a topical analgesic, if you need it. I shall turn you onto your back and make the sign of The Cross over your face and body. I shall aloud beg Our Holy Savior to forgive you your evils, to remit any further penalty they may have accrued, to accept your Sacrifice of suffering as Imitation of Christ, and to strengthen you against further sinning. Finally, I shall kiss you and leave you to rise and dress in your own good time. I shall perform this rite regardless of your sex or your beliefs. If you are uncomfortable with any part of this procedure you may request that it is abridged or omitted.

<u>After your Correction</u>

Your bottom will feel very sore and hot. Dressing will be uncomfortable, but a cooling spray or ointment, ibuprofen and an antihistamine will be available to you if you desire them. The inflammation will disappear overnight. I will try to avoid any bruising action, either of blows or grip, but some kinds of medication or disease conditions may make you prone to bruises. Any bruises may take some days to disappear and be tender for a time. No mark or weal will remain anywhere. If you bathe topical analgesia will of course be re-applied.

After a day or two I shall email or call you to see if you are okay and ask whether or not you have derived any benefit from our meeting. You will not be pressured to repeat the process, though of course I will be amenable if you wish to arrange a future Correction. This is your opportunity to highlight any issues that arose with my organisation or management, and to offer suggestions for improvement.

You may feel that whilst Holy Correction does not suit you, you nevertheless wish to maintain contact. My door is always open to you, and I would be delighted to see you again for gentle prayer and study.

<u>Our Sacred Covenant</u>

If once you have bared to me your body and soul and lain across my lap then there is a Sacred Covenant between us. This Sacred Covenant is a bond of trust. It is forever. It is not a contract that men can enforce for no man made it. No oath can blaspheme our Covenant nor any decree revoke. This is for you and me. God has brought it to us. It is for God to forbear or exact at Will.

It is a new star in the firmament of human relationships: Original, eternal, resplendent and self-subsistent.

It has nothing to do with attraction, approval, interest, intellectual assent or any other form of liking between us. It is not, of itself, love. Even if neither of us were to believe in Christ or God, or either, then God would Witness our Covenant he Made. God tutored us. God watches our tottering steps. God Waits.

I am happy to hold you without hitting you, to hear you, and to help if I can. We met alone in secret and entrusted one another with our Mortal Lives and our Immortal Souls, under God's Gaze. We survived and arose cleansed and refreshed, ready to repair our depredations. It is enough. On your part our sacred trust commits you to one obligation only: If I call to confess my sin, you will honor me a like service, without deputation, demurral or disgust, and to the best of your beliefs and abilities.

Your Way

Psychological and spiritual effects are likely to be much more persistent than the physical. They may even be lifelong, even if whilst finding your experience positive and beneficial you nevertheless decide that a repetition is unnecessary.

Oxytocin response and other beneficial hormonal toning may persist for days in males and weeks in females. These are natural effects in apes subjected to social violence. You will feel very contented, trusting and ready to believe the best of life and the people around you. You will tend to be religious, gentle and reverential in your emotional and intellectual dispositions. Such responses may persist for a long time and return unexpectedly, especially after sexual stimulation. This is the essentially physiological outcome aimed at by sadomasochists and LDD enthusiasts.

With time, this response is likely to mature to a higher state, similar to the love of a parent for her child, or the love between committed sexual partners, but if so is likely to remain as a more diffuse, unprojected wellbeing. This is the best most us can hope for. I am sorry about the language and the clinical tone, but it is in everyone's interests to be realistic.

Your spiritual and ethical growth, if any, is much more momentous, and what this whole exercise is really about.

You may attain, but cannot aim at, a higher supernatural ecstasy or epiphany that will change your thought and behaviour radically and for the better. Such would lead to dramatic changes in your personal happiness and capability. This effect is due to a direct confrontation with Evil, and its extirpation with Divine assistance. You will forgive your enemies and yourself, remove the obstructions and temptations that caused your problems in the first place, and move on with your life confident in the support of God and your own abilities to cope. This is the kind of thing the prophets and saints of old wrote about, and sometimes experienced for themselves.

Your mind and face shall transfigure. No task or tribulation shall daunt you, nor any spite dismay. Your friends and colleagues will wonder at the change. Few will surmise its origin, and none guess its instance.

Your Act of Trust is yours, a free gift to you from the God of your Heart, inalienable and indefeasible, and a precious part of your developing self-mastery. If you will forgive the attenuated metaphor, it is as if by some strange alchemy you transmute the hot, the frantic and the saturnine into a moonlit solace of the cool, the calm and the serene, basking in beams thrice reflected to a blue balm.

The acolytes of Satan will give you a wide berth. So, more regrettably, will committed Marxists and other good if mistaken men, people that you might wish to be with you, even to share your bliss. Do not worry. Their time will come. Treat them pleasantly and pray in your heart.

The good man who made me turn to Christ was a communist, and the man who inspired me to do this service is the health and safety officer in a BDSM dungeon. Okay, I accept that you do not believe me: Jim, it is his little joke, no? Well, neither would they believe you if you told them why you had changed. They would think you mocked them.

It is our responsibility to grasp evil and amend it to good if life is to persist on this planet.

You will not bring justice to either friend or foe, because that is beyond mortal gift. But you will bless and favor all with cheerful kindness and tender regard. Old wrongs will not be forgotten but ill will shall evaporate in a new dawn of warm contentment, because forgiveness is contagious.

Your life will be a voiceless prayer. Paul told us to pray without surcease (First Thessalonians 5:17) and Our Holy Savior not to do penance solemnly or with ostentation, but with a wash, a smile, and an easy manner as we go about our business (Matthew 6:16-18).

All scepticism will be cast aside, but your intellectual and emotional acuities shall be sharper than ever, and your doubts a source of new and vibrant understanding. Life is paradox.

Sanctity is a taste of Eden and your first toddling step to Paradise.

Thank you for reading this chapter. We are now nearly at its end. I know that it was as tough for you to read it as it was for me to write. If after all you still do not take spanking seriously, that is okay: Spanking is silly. It is only a means to an end: To help you love more, abhor evil and treat those around you with greater compassion. The part which is desperately, utterly, compellingly serious is the sacred. You and I must love goodness with mind and spirit; detect, identify and abhor evil; exploit evil against itself; and be merciful.

These things must be done, severally and collectively. The price of failure is the extinction of our species.

One day long ago another took such a walk. He struck out for a city beyond the sands, his mind set on cruelty. The road was long and hard, and the Sun shone mercilessly. Robbers and rapists abounded, and a Roman passport gave no protection from them. We do not know whether Saul took a hiding of the flesh for he is silent about low things. Certainly his few companions reported nothing. We do know that in his hunger and his guilt and his thirst and his shame he had a great epiphany. He cast aside bigotry and sin, for that is what Pride and Wrath are.

After his conversion Saul assumed the name Paul.

Later he met some Corinthian friends (First Corinthians 1:17-28) and speaking of The Crucifixion of Christ he reminded them that Greeks sought wisdom whereas Jews looked for revelation. He added that to Jews, who thought hanged men accursed, the Cross was a stumbling block, whilst to the Greeks the Cross was foolishness. But, Paul continued, the foolishness of God is wiser than man; and the weakness of God stronger than men (First Corinthians 1:25).

Life is strange. Go with God.

CHAPTER SEVEN
JANE'S CORRECTION

In several ways Jane's Correction exemplified a very ordinary but entirely satisfactory Sacrament from which I flatter myself that she benefited mightily. Certainly, Jane was a great delight to her Confessor, and I trust that I returned to her children and her workmates a truly superb woman, better than the excellent woman I found, and a shining tribute to the Love of her Creator.

But I really do flatter myself: All the good work was hers, and she strove for her greatness. Her travail and her gain were magnificent. Certainly there was no transverberation, whatever that is: At least I do not think there was. But there was surprise, delight, and a workwoman-like repair of broken bridges.

Of course I am well aware that our circumstances reflect much wider social and economic problems, a great nation's anastomosing, ramified and seemingly intractable failures and injustices that individuals are trapped and dis-fulfilled by. There is the backdrop of Britain's absolute monarchy, signally ill-fitted for a modern age, and the nation's well-known and well-canvassed inadequacies. But these great affairs cannot be my concern. I am a seventy-three year old diabetic myasthenial with a dislocated shoulder. I must do what I can, as they say at Stonyhurst. As has also been said, if every man does all he can, and every man is true, individuals might achieve significant mitigations of the collective agony. I paraphrase of course, but I am sure you get the picture.

Once again, I apologise for the tone and the language, but we have to be frank about these things.

It is profitless to dismiss "Jane's Correction" as fiction or pornography. Rather it serves as an epitome and a prospectus of the loveliness of rigorous confession, of its catharsis, its cleansing and of its empowerment.

Of course Jane is not my Penitent's real name. And her history is *sub rosa* for Confessions are deeply secret and individuals, I trust, unidentifiable. But her story though composite and typical is nevertheless glorious, and the lessons she teaches salutary.

Jane worked for Bonnard plc (formerly & Co.Ltd.), one of those over-conservative UK manufacturing firms in the thick-film IC sector. You must forgive me if I garble the facts. Electronics is not my specialism. But it was Jane's. She held four science degrees, including a doctorate in electrical engineering from Imperial College, the UK's leading technical university. Her research subject had been quantum electrodynamics. Like me, she had formerly been active in the murkier reaches of the St James', London, consultancy world. Also like me, she lost her livelihood and her prospects when British heavy industry evaporated in the Thatcher years.

I digress.

When Jane first contacted me she was fifty-eight years old and tentatively communicated via pseudonymous emails. She was exercised by what she clearly thought a great offence and, being a religious woman unimpressed with the existing conformities, seemed to wonder if confessing to me might help.

Jane was working as one of a team of fabricators on a bench in one of the heterodyne workshops of Bonnard's when she fell into an altercation with her immediate line manager about the alleged inadequacy of her, Jane's, work. Jane's supervisor, Mary (let us call her) stated that the failure rate of Jane's inspected circuits was marginally unacceptable. It seemed to me, rightly or wrongly, that there was an underlying history of jealousy or animus between the two women.

Anyway, to cut a long and not especially enlightening story short, Jane called Mary a "stupid fat pig." Jane flounced out to calm herself in the nearest Wetherspoon's whilst Mary spent the rest of the morning crying in the factory's ladies' loo. The effects on a Jane habitually teetotal are better imagined than described. Mary complained to the Management. Whether that Management was intelligent enough to entertain the obvious ideas that occurred to you and I we know not, but the upshot was that Bonnard's Human Resources Officer handed Jane a Written Warning. British procedure, almost never honoured of course, is to give two Written Warnings before dismissal on the third offence. This was Jane's second current Warning. No union was recognised at Bonnard's, only the tame Staff Association. But, regrettably, any union would have been perfectly useless.

To clarify a slightly technical point that Jane used to rationalise her offence or exculpate herself during the less healthy seasons of her guilt I should relay the following facts as I understand them. There were three main departments or "bays" in the Ilford factory: The ECG Section where heterodynes were made for fitting into electrocardiograph assemblies. Here for all the obvious reasons quality control was stringent and a theoretical 0.001% failure rate tolerated, though in practice a Japanese-style TQC philosophy was in effect; the second department was the Theremin Section, where Jane worked, and the control level was five percent. A theremin is a sort of electronic harp that in expert hands can create sonatas of eerie quartertones; then there was the Mines Section where heterodynes were made for incorporation in military and recreational metal detectors.

For some weeks Jane and I exchanged emails in which we discussed background, procedures and protocols. We also hammered-out prayer and reading schedules, on the explicit understanding that we both had licence to vary these in the event.

We set aside a whole afternoon knowing that the spanking Reparation phase was likely to be over in minutes: It actually span-out into a much longer observance though thankfully with only moderate violence.

One rainy Saturday afternoon Jane turned up in my Sanctuary.

She cut a most elegant figure of middle-aged intellectual Quaker ladyhood in her expensive closely-tailored black dress with a white collared blouse, and with a pair of sensible shoes. She had obviously made an effort. Thick, grey-blonde hair tumbled about her head and chest. There was not a sign of metalwork or make-up. It was difficult to believe that this woman would insult anyone, much less use profane language in a holy sacrament.

Meanwhile, I strode forward with all the bald and corpulent grace of Mr Danny De Vito, but none of his homely charm or finesse. I was clad only in my floral silk dressing-gown.

Jane proffered a sinewed but refined hand and looked into my eyes with a frank and slightly foxy gaze I thought, but with neither pudor nor arrogance.

"It is good to meet you at last, Dr Warren", Jane said.

"Please call me Jim", I replied.

"How do you do, Jim"

"My boss, Mary, came to me and said I had wired 5.2 percent of our widgets defectively. The control threshold is five percent. I called her a stupid fat pig. She spent the rest of the morning crying in the lavatory. HR have given me a written warning", continued Jane breathlessly, though of course I was already across this.

Taking her hand I confided, "I have just had a shower." Perhaps this was a kind of apology for my undress (notwithstanding that we had agreed I could work naked), perhaps to buy time. I do not really know why. Perhaps I was just nervous.

"Oh, poor Jane", I said solicitously, "But more so poor Mary. Let's pray for her, and later maybe help God to make her happy again. Please undress, Jane, not forgetting your jewellery, and I will sit on the couch. You will lie across my thighs, tummy down."

As I have remarked, I did not see any jewellery on Jane and would not expect any on one of her religion, but I was kind of working on autopilot.

Without reply, but after a smile and a firming of her handshake, Jane placed her clothing on a nearby chair and sought the bathroom. "It is over there", I gestured off-handedly as I busied-about placing a plastic cup of refrigerated sparkling water on the little table by the head, together with the jelly-babies she wanted, our printed prayers, and our KJV prepared with Post-It® tabs. (The gelatine of the jelly babies was made from soybean: Jane had checked). I re-checked my medicines case and pushed it beneath the couch. I checked the charge of my cellphone and then turned it off. I removed my gown and resumed my seat on the couch, plumping the pillows for Jane's head and placing one over my crotch, not in false delicacy, but to raise her pelvis and shield her from any, now sadly unlikely, tumidity.

Presently, I helped Jane settle across my lap, and cupped my left hand across her waist. Her skin was still damp from the shower, and I realised the blows would be especially painful unless I moderated them, which I determined to do. Despite the odd mole and mark of age her skin was fine and her toned figure robust without flabbiness anywhere. Only on her round and womanly bottom was there a trace of cellulite which pleased with childish dimples, rather than the grossness of decline. The impression was one not of athleticism or affectation but of a healthy abstinent veganism and regular but useful exercise.

Gently taking her right wrist in my left hand and holding both to her waist I asked as formality dictated, "What would you wish to say to me, Madam?"

A strange chivalry attends consensual spanking: It is a safeguard as well as an ornament.

"Holy Confessor, I called my supervisor a 'stupid fat pig'."

"Is that a sin?" I responded, I hope without sarcasm.

There was momentary confusion, and I thought some hesitation.

"I hurt my boss and made her cry", replied Jane.

"I am going to hurt you and make you cry. Where is the sin?" I said.

"My sins are the mortal spites of pride and anger. Pride that I am better than she, notwithstanding that I am not, and anger at her resented censure."

My initial impression that I was confronted with a creature of quality was now confirmed one thousand fold and I looked down upon her with a sort of superstitious trepidation.

"Dr Mayfield, are you comfortable?" I enquired. With a man I would probably just have asked if he was ready (for the blows), but I am too conservative to invite a woman to a corporal act.

Surprisingly, this enquiry only elicited a murine little squeak from the subject.

"Jane, you are a very brave woman. Please answer me clearly and firmly as you have always spoken to me before."

"Yes, Sir. And I am comfortable."

I thought to myself, *"I am not going to reprove her honorifics. If they make her happy or confident I will put up with them."*

"Say this prayer aloud", I said.

> **My Holy Savior**
> **Guard and keep the purity**
> > **of my confessor James**
> **Let him enjoy**
> > **no profane delight**
> **In my pain or exposure**
> **Make him shrive me**
> > **with apt words and**
> > **sincere prayers**
> **Timely, prudent and useful**
> **And let him strike without**
> > **stint and without spite**
> **But with completeness and**
> > > **compassion**
> > **Please help him God**
> > > ***Please help me God***

I paused after each line to help her memory.
Then I said this:-

> **My Holy Savior**
> **Award your daughter**
> > **Jane fortitude**
> **The courage to endure**
> > **and the strength to pray**
> **Let her pain be light and**
> > **the chastening of**
> > **her spirit complete**
> **Take her sin and set it**
> > **at naught**
> **Restore to her the**

**Innocency that her
trespass adulterated
Forgive her now and forever
And prompt the forgiveness
of those she wronged
Please help her God**
Please help me God

I am ashamed to admit that I had to read it to get it right. Then I said:-

"We will do a breathing exercise, Jane. When I say 'in' you will inhale deeply; when I say 'out' you will exhale as completely as you can, on the third 'out' I will strike your bottom very hard ten times. Do you understand?"

"Yes, Sir"

Then I rained the ten blows hard and fast with my right hand. Her lower buttocks flushed red. Jane whimpered and her breaths were shallow and irregular.

Jane squirmed slightly down couch and under her breath I heard her say:-

"Oh, fuck"

"Please don't say that", I objected softly, but you may think sanctimoniously. "The thing you traduced is a very holy thing. It was the first thing God told us to do. Without it we could not make the babies who love us all our lives, and then beyond the grave."

"Sorry, Sir", replied Jane, as she began to sob more bitterly.

I had rested my right hand on her thigh to avoid irritating her hot, sore bottom. I gave her a gentle squeeze of acceptance.

"My good woman, and you are a very good woman, whatever you may think, have a really good cry. Your courage and your tenacity are not in doubt, so why play the stoic? The last person you need to impress is Jim Warren so let your tears flow like the falls of Tivoli. They will wash the anger, the frustration and the bitterness right out of your soul. Do not think I am patronising you because you are a woman: I would say the same to any man on my lap. Except I would call him a 'good man' rather than a 'good woman': I am not foolishly brave."

This rider provoked a brief laugh from my fair Penitent, before she reverted to her over-controlled sobbing. I was glad I had provoked a flash of cheer. I hoped there would be more.

Placing my hands under her armpits I slid her awkwardly back into position.

I said:-

"We will now have a quiet few moments to gather our thoughts. Try to pray if you can, Honey Pet. You are a real woman. And you are a fine figure of one", I added insolently, but sincerely.

Then Jane said:-

My Dear Lord Jesus…,

and paused as she sobbed and whimpered.

"Take your time, Love", I said quietly.

> **My Dear Lord Jesus**
> **Thank you for**
> **this firm, frank man**
> **His sound correction and**
> **His sage and sacred counsel…**

I ought to have said "That is quite enough of that!" but I could not bring myself to put her down. Her little prayer was well meant and addressed to Someone Else.

I patted that luxuriant silver-gilt hair at the back of her head with my now-redundant left hand.

What I actually said was:-

"What about poor Mary! She only tried to help you by warning you about your work before the Management found out about it, and you repaid her with spite, insult and humiliation."

Of course, I did not know whether this was strictly true, and I cared even less. What I cared about was the woman lying naked across my lap, her Act of Trust, and our mutual Witness under God. Somehow, against all my inclination, I found myself defending a woman I had never met, and would probably dislike if I did. Mary seemed to me, perhaps quite unfairly, to be a quitter. I mis-trust quitters. She quit her workshop to hide in the lavatory. Then she quit her underling, abandoning her to the mercies of administrators, notorious abdicationalists all.

"Sod Mary! She is a complete fuckwit!" was the startlingly venomous response.

"Please try to control your anger, lovely Friend", I softly admonished, "You are an intelligent and very brave woman who deserves better than the fare with which she serves herself. Mary is a diligent and helpful woman who is only trying to do her job whilst protecting yourself and the other girls under her charge."

Remember, reader, that whilst all this profane backchat was going on both Jane and I were supposedly still under the discipline of Reparation.

"And even if she is a fuckwit", I continued, "Surely it is your place, as an older and much more able and educated woman to make her life as easy as possible, lifting some of the load of responsibility she bears, trapped and ground as she is between the upper stone of the Management and the nether of her operatives."

Jane's sobbing had moderated and she was showing further signs of anger and some physiological distress. Her face had flushed red whilst her body had blanched in morbid sudation.

"She had no right to complain about one in five hundred superadded defectives. The customers can always complain if they cannot get the tone they need. We are only making gizmos for thylacines for fuck's sake", warbled my Penitent in unreconstructed wrath.

"Can we complain if we fail to get the tone we need?" I asked glibly.

Being a bit slow and rather emotional myself I was initially confused by this outburst. Did she mean "thylacines" (*Thylacinus cynocephalus*), extinct marsupial dogs. Then I thought in my obtuse way that in her confusion and distress she must have meant theramine or something.

"Do you mean theramines, Jane?"

The decumbent woman turned a swift scowl to me. Then she burst into hysterical, almost diabolic, laughter.

I was not certain. I wondered if I should postpone the Sacrament. I made a silent, inchoate prayer, I suppose for Guidance. I did not like the tendency of this interview. I did not like my management of it. I was not here to indulge in arguments with near-strangers or to participate in profanity or malicious gossip.

Then I said:-

"Jane, you are very courageous woman and I am going to give you some more strikes. I know you can take them and use them for your own purposes. Please, please believe me: This is not a punishment for swearing, or because you hate Mary, or for anything at all. This is for your penance and your prayer. I suppose it is like a boost to rocket you onto a higher level of spiritual perspective, if that makes sense. There will be about twenty-four hard spanks, probably balanced between each cheek. But please do *not* count. Please try to relax and to pray if you can. Pray for the animals who suffer so much and whom I know you love so much."

Jane became strangely still and passive. She did not comment or reply. She did not request a rite of clemency neither did she deploy her safeword. I did not offer, nor did she request, a breathing exercise.

I rained the blows hard and fast.

After initial silence, Jane screamed in a volcanic access of pain, and then fell to a steady, tortured sobbing into her pillows.

My dislocated shoulder had started grinding and groaning audibly as it sometimes does after heavy load. There was no pain. After all, it is mostly metal and plastic. But three of my digits and my palm were smarting terribly, and the numbness that I often suffer in my thumb and index finger had returned with a vengeance. The arthritis in my wrist was excruciating. But there should be pain for the confessor too. It is moderating and condign. It is another excellent argument for using no instrument.

Then a strange question entered my head, as if from nowhere. Did Jesus Christ ever suffer a pain in the wrist, and if so why?

The moral and physical pain that Jane was suffering was nearly unbearable, and her cataclysm of anguish continued. We could only wait.

This episode of actual spanking would have taken no more than thirty seconds, perhaps nearer twenty-five. But it seemed an hour to me, and would have been much longer to Jane.

I had not reckoned with the depth of Jane's hate. This could go either way. Naively, I wondered why if Jane felt this way she would wish to confess any offence directed at Mary. I had not encountered anything precisely like this. Instinctively I felt that further beating was somehow inappropriate, perhaps even counterproductive.

"*I cannot hit this woman again*", I thought.

Then I had an idea. I reached for the Bible and found Psalm 37:8-11 and slowly, all but whispered the calming verses to Jane.

"Jane?" I then asked, "Is this true? Shall those who forsake wrath and wait on the Lord, shall they inherit the Earth?"

Jane hesitated in perplexed silence.

"I don't know, Jim. If God says so it must be true", she conceded at last.

"If a woman like you does not know, then what hope is there that I or Mary should understand? We must all wait on the Lord."

Then I said:-

"Jane, can weaklings inherit the Earth?"

"Huh?" said Jane in surprised dismission, "I doubt such could inherit anything."

"So you are saying that the meek are strong?" I pressed my cod syllogism. "Jane, draw not your sword to cast down poor Mary. Rather be strong and forsake anger and resentment. Use your courage and your understanding and your prayer and your Faith to be meek and strong, and at peace. Help Mary and conserve and prosper everyone's livelihoods, even in these bleak days."

I continued:-

"Satan hates people who are meek, mature and self-confident. He much prefers weak people whom he can manipulate, because he is a coward and a bully himself. Are you a bully, Jane?"

Suddenly, abruptly enough to make me start in alarm, Jane burst into almost hysterical weeping.

"No, …no, …no, Master", she gasped, or I should say brayed.

As I reached for the duvet with my damaged right arm, the same that I had spanked her with, I gently turned her supine and raised her on my lap. I folded the cover about her to assuage her developing chill. She cast her arms around my neck to support herself. In this very intimate position I stole a dry chaste kiss upon her lips, and I said:-

"Please repeat this prayer of gratitude line by line after me":-

> **My Holy Savior,**
> **accept my tears as my**
> **Sacred Pledge of Contrition**
> **Let the water wash my spirit**
> **and relent to disclose a**
> **sunlit land of Holy Content**
> **In a blameless life**
> **restored to me**

Jane delicately did as bidden in her lovely lisping contralto voice.

Then I said:-

> **My Holy Savior,**
> **comfort your suffering**
> **daughter Jane**
> **Let her know that**
> **through her anguish**
> **A larger light shall dawn**
> **Magnified through**
> **her clear tears**

Continuing very softly, I said:-

"Please, My Revered Friend Jane, say this special prayer with Jim as our only Lord, Jesus Christ taught us." [Matthew 6:9-13]:-

Our Father,

which art in heaven,

hallowed be thy name;

thy kingdom come;

thy will be done,

in earth as it is in heaven.

Give us this day

our daily bread.

And forgive us

our trespasses,

as we forgive them

that trespass against us.

And lead us not

into temptation;

but deliver us from evil.

For thine is the kingdom,

the power, and the glory,

For ever and ever.

Amen.

I was still cuddling Jane on the sofa. Her sweating and her morbid facial flush had subsided. Her pulse rate had fallen. I gently divested her of the duvet, as tenderly and as reverently as I could. I picked up the sparkling water cup, and offered it to her. I also was naked and my scarred limbs and torso fully exposed. I said:-

"Please take a few deep swigs of this."

Jane obliged. Then, taking the empty vessel from her I said:-

"Do you wish to visit the lavatory?"

"No, Sir"

"Jane, I want you to be a very, very brave young woman. Will you be a very brave young woman, just for Jim?"

"Are you going to spank me again?" Jane enquired with an anxious face.

"Jane, we are still in Reparation, even this late in the Sacrament. Your Penance is your pain and your prayer. You may only ask questions to clarify the character of your sin and its proscriptions. You have not voiced The Act of Contrition. You are not ready for it. Please resume the position."

"Oh, please, Holy Master, please don't spank me. I am very sore. Please spare me", begged the poor woman, gazing tearfully into my eyes and wringing her elegant hands.

Many of my male readers will find it extraordinary that a woman as bold and assertive, and as aged and accomplished, as Jane Mayfield should suddenly abase herself in this manner. After all, she could exercise her safeword at any time. This is to misunderstand the spiritual and psychosexual female desire for immersive and intimate submission. Hers was not an act of conscious manipulation and it had even less to do with the political or religious doctrines of the individual concerned, if any. But it did, in some profound way, reflect a sexual and a spiritual need.

"Please, My Pet. Lovely, brave Jane. I thought you were such a steadfast, honest, steady woman. Please do not undeceive me", I begged, settling back to my seated posture, with the pillow over my genitals.

Slowly, deliberately, Jane settled back across my thighs, blanched and fell silent.

Every muscle in her body seemed as tight as a tide-tensed hawser. Especially her gluteal muscles.

Jane had resumed a steady sobbing.

I started to speak again. It was not textbook ministry of course. I doubt if either of us would have emerged sane if we had stilled our tongues.

"I know you are brave", I continued, "I know you can fight. But you do not need to fight. This is not the occasion. Just give up. Try to relax, my Lovely Friend."

"You hated the woman your hate had made you. You asked God to make you the woman He wanted you to be. You asked me to help God. I too readily judge. My experience has proven my judgement ever defective. I asked God to take the judgmentality from me. I asked God to lead my hand. You cannot trust Jim Warren. You must trust God. God is handing down His Judgment upon us."

"Remember, my gentle Darling, the Ministry of Our Holy Savior" [Matthew 6:34]:-

Take therefore no thought
for the morrow:
for the morrow shall take
thought for the
things of itself.
Sufficient unto the day
is the evil thereof.

I gently stroked the small of her back, and extended the caresses to the rest of her back, alternating the pressures slightly.

I clasped the cheeks of her bottom firmly, rubbed and massaged them.

"Jane, say these words after me":-

Master of Masters
 Master of Masters
Whose yoke is easy and
 whose burden is light
 Whose yoke is easy and
 whose burden is light
Help us share our burdens
 that we may keep
 Help us share our
 burdens
 that we may keep
The Law of Christ
 The Law of Christ
Make us also meek and lowly
 in heart
 Make us also meek and
 lowly in heart
That rest may be unto
 our souls
 That rest may be unto
 our souls

Master, load me
your daughter Jane
Master, load me
your daughter Jane
With a little of Mary's Load
With a little of
Mary's Load
That She and I may
walk in comradeship
That She and I may
walk in comradeship
That I may
Support and Love
That I may
Support and Love
Putting behind me all
jealousy and spite
Putting behind me all
jealousy and spite
Master of Masters
Master of Masters
Where I scowled let me smile
Where I scowled
let me smile
Where I complained
let me commend
Where I complained
let me commend
Where I harmed let me heal
Where I harmed
let me heal
Where Mary stumbles,
    let me speed to her aid

Where Mary stumbles,
let me speed
to her aid

Master, make me crush
my pride for metal
Master, make me
crush my pride for metal
On the rocky road ahead
On the rocky road ahead
Amen
Amen

I continued to stroke the flesh of her bottom and her thighs, more gently and slowly than before. Much of the hot ruddiness had subsided.

Sometime during this prayer Jane relaxed. I think she realised that the spanking was finished with: Perhaps for the rest of her mortal life. Her fabric visibly loosened. I felt her gluteal folds. They had resumed a healthy malleability. I gave the right one a cheeky little pinch.

Jane flinched and giggled in delight.

"Jane, you are a woman" I said with a certain unfortunate interrogative inflexion to my portent.

"I certainly hope so, Sir"

We dissolved into a cooling squall of shared laughter.

When I had gathered my wits I continued:-

"Tell me this, have I abused, degraded or demeaned you? As a woman, I mean?"

"Absolutely not, James"

"Have I dishonoured or disrespected you, James, as a man or as a minister?"

I was abashed by this question, by its directness, and about what I unreasonably thought an almost obscene redundancy.

"In no manner", I at last replied.

"How do you feel?" I enquired.

"Fantastic"

The rain had passed and fitful partings permitted diffident shafts of sunlight.

I stretched over Jane's prone form. Somehow she seemed, if possible, more shapely, more refined, more beautiful and yet at the same time more elderwomanly. Just then the setting sun broke through the overburden and slanted through the clerestory, gilding her fair selenian flesh with its happy warm light.

Another weird idea crossed my mind. Her late husband must have thought himself Endymion.

I retrieved the medicine case from under the couch and removed the remote control. I opened two panes of the clerestory windows. Suddenly the late afternoon birdsong became audible, as also distant trains and traffic. A cold zephyr raced across us causing the bathroom light cord's plastic knob to tap against the tiling and the window frames to tick contractively.

As I looked up to adjudge the aperture I was struck by the strangely smoky impression of the side-lit ceiling fresco as the declining rays obliquely struck it. It reminded me of the aurous rays of a Roman winter's sun gilding the golden throne of St Peter's in the peopled and dusty Vatican of my youth. It was a fine modern rendition, apparently in acrylics, of a standing Christ with a miniature cross cradled in his right arm and a red rose in his left hand. A circlet of golden stars garlanded his dis-tortured head like a nimbus. I thought it a fine and modest painting, a soothing consolation to any penitent resting supine, though of course usually overlooked by anyone prone or seated.

How apt the iconography, I thought, for our sacred and confidential order, a small and secret society, gentle and rigorous, and by another grand paradox, open and accessible to all.

Jane lay prone and very quiet. I think she may have been sleepy. Certainly I felt tired but also very serene. I began to feel her weight on my thighs. A strange catharsis, I was going to write "a strange catharsis descended" but somehow that is the wrong expression, somehow too kinetic. A strange peace like a forming immanence seemed, so to say, to precipitate in the air around us, like a mist at sea.

"Jane, are you ready for The Act of Contrition?" I asked.

"Yes, Grand Master"

"Please don't call me that, Dr Mayfield", I replied with all the pompous severity I could muster, "I am conceited enough already."

"There is little reason your bottom should hurt any longer. Would you like some analgesic?"

"Only a topical rub, Jim, please"

"Okay. I will give you a 2% racemic menthol gel rub on your bottom, on your perineum and in your intergluteal cleft. It will feel thrillingly cold. After your shower I will give you an ibuprofen rub that should give you a comfortable night."

"Whatever you think is best, Jim"

I administered the soothing ointment.

"Jane, say this after me", I continued:-

My Dear God,
    I am sorry for my sins
    with all my heart.
In choosing to do wrong
    and failing to do good,

I have sinned against
> You whom I should
> love above all things.
I hate my sin and
> *I reject it with loathing.*
I firmly intend, with
> Your help, to use
> the pain of penance
To sin no more,
> and to avoid
> whatever leads me to sin.
Your Son,
> Jesus Christ, suffered
> and died for us.
In His name,
> my God, have mercy.
> Amen

My Penitent rehearsed this prayer in a meek and contrite spirit. Naturally, I fed her the lines one at a time.
Then I recited this:-

My Holy Savior
Accept I beg you
The pain of your daughter
> **Jane as Reparation**
> **for her Sin**
Remove all distress from
> **her mind and spirit**
Prepare her to amend and
> **recompense her evil**
And please exact
> **no further penalty on Earth**

Or in The Life to Come

And with that Pledge and that Plea Restoration technically commenced.

The sky was clearing. I was distinctly chill. I do not know whether it was the stress, my low blood sugar, the gathering blue-skied vespertide, or some combination of the three. I picked up the remote control and closed the windows again. I was starting to tremble.

I picked up the duvet and spread it over Jane.

I said, "Please rise and sit beside me."

As Jane sat beside me she cast aside the cover. Her body now had a healthy all-over light blush.

"I prefer to be naked before my God and before my confessor", averred Jane, "It is my earnest of good faith."

"Thank you, Jane", I answered, "Please may I put on my dressing gown? I feel cold."

"Of course you may, Jim"

I fumbled inside the refrigerated console. I fished out some fresh crusty bread rolls, wonderful for making a plastic sofa uninhabitable; and a bottle of good Rioja.

"Is there gelatine or isinglass in that?" my Penitent enquired severely.

"I am sorry, Jane, I do not know", I admitted.

I put two clean tumblers on the console top, and poured us draughts, in theory seventy-five milliliters each. I then broke a roll and solemnly gave part of it to Jane with the wine in its glass. I sat beside her with my bread and wine.

"Master, is this the token of Sacrifice that Our Lord taught us?" said Jane with soft reverence. There is no Eucharist in Quakerdom, and she was maybe anxious not to mistake the occasion.

"Please do not speak, Honey Pet", I replied, "There are good reasons for silence, reasons schooled in blood and fire. Please be still. When we are ready I shall ask you to teach me the lesson you have prepared."

I do not know how long our simple meal lasted. Maybe five minutes; maybe fifteen. We both prayed silently, and wept quietly.

When we had finished, and opened our tearful eyes to smile upon each other, I said to Jane:-

"Please read me your condign lesson, Beautiful."

Jane picked up the Bible and turned to First Corinthians 13, a popular choice but never trite, and, I thought, very apt to our context. Jane spoke distinctly and clearly in her lovely, authoritative cadence. When she reached the Eighth Verse I burst into fluid tears:-

Charity never faileth:
but
whether there be prophecies,
they shall fail;
whether there be tongues,
they shall cease;
whether there be knowledge,
it shall vanish away.

I am an old scientist. If my life has taught me anything, it is this.

Jane grasped my hand, squeezed, and continued unfalteringly to the end of the chapter.

After Jane had finished her reading, I read her Ruth Chapter Two.

"Thank you for your Ministry", said Jane with a solemn countenance and down-cast eyes.

"It was a great pleasure, and a great honour, Jane." I opened the draw of the console and removing something I gave it to Jane. It was a simple silver crucifix on a neck chain.

"Jane", I said, "I know you don't wear jewellery but please wear this to my funeral in memory of me."

Jane burst into abandoned crying, and placed the emblem about her neck. I embraced her.

Again time slipped by. In some deeply unknowable way time does not exist. To the eternal a second may as well be an hour or a day, and the Days of Creation a myriad eons.

"Jane", I said, "I wish to deconstruct the insult you cast at Mary."

Jane giggled uncertainly.

"First of all the pig (*Sus scrufa*)"

"That is the Eurasian Wild Boar", Jane specified.

"She is the one", I confirmed.

"She is intelligent and brave, sedulous to guard and tend her sounder, and feed her babes, willing to lose her life that they might live. A good husbandwoman, ploughing no land to exhaustion, and as ready to eat an acorn or a gall as a truffle or a rose. She helps and protects the other sows about her. Is Mary like that?" I asked earnestly.

Jane shrieked with astonished laughter, and then became suddenly silent. After a moment, with seriousness Jane said, "Yes, I suppose she is."

"So you like pigs?" I asked Jane.

"Yea, they're great! You should stop eating them", Jane said pointedly.

"One day before I die I shall call and tell you to correct my manifold cruelties", I responded.

Jane suddenly sobered-up.

"Is she fat?" I enquired.

"Oh, undeniably!" was Jane's assessment, "There is a group photo of her with Bonnard brass on the company website. You should check it out!" Jane added with jolly triumph. "Am I fat, Jane", I rejoindered. Jane hesitated. Then she said diffidently, but distinctly, "Yes, Master."

"Well, I was going to suggest you send her a box of chocolates as a peace offering. Perhaps we should skip that idea. She might think we were compounding the insult!" I advised light-heartedly.

Jane laughed. "Yes, I think something else would be more tactful. But not cake!" she agreed.

"And what about stupid?"

"No, Mary is not that", Jane stated solemnly, "She has few academic qualifications. I think the best is an Open University degree in physics, but she knows her job and does it meticulously."

"I think you rather like Mary", I said.

Jane burst into tears again. I wondered how long she could sustain this emotional roller-coaster, physiologically I mean. She was no chicken. Neither was I a kid.

"I tell you again, my much respected woman, that Satan does not like meek, mature, self-confident people. He hates you. You are evading his grasp. And there is nothing he can do about it", I said almost painfully to her left ear, as now I found myself cuddling her like an ardent adolescent.

"This is what I want you to do", I said.

"Yes, Jim, anything. What is it?"

"I want you to put your clothes back on and I want you to go over to the desk and sit down on your bottom which I know is still very sore and I want you to write a nice letter to Mary apologising for your spiteful, arrogant, self-indulgent, wicked behavior and promising for the future to be helpful, cheerful, courteous, obedient and kind, and specifying that you wish to rectify the poor and shoddy work you offered. Then I want you to address it to Mary with honorific formality obviously and put it in an envelope marked 'Private and Confidential' with a first-class stamp and addressed to Mrs Mary Michaels BSc(Hons), Bonnard plc, 43 Maitliss Road, London IG7 4GF."

"But before you seal the envelope I wish to read and if appropriate approve your letter."

"Then I wish you to get your credit card and use my landline to ring InterFlora® and order them to send a £100 mixed bouquet of red roses and golden roses to Mrs Mary Michaels at Bonnard's to arrive at 1100 on Monday morning."

"Do you have any questions?"

"No, Master. I shall do all that you say. Before I do so may I make an observation, Sir?"

"Yes you may Jane. What is it?"

"In all our intercourse this is the only humiliation I have suffered at your hand."

I bowed at Jane with a sullen Teutonic correctness.

"May I reply Madam?" I asked coldly.

"Yes, you may" said Jane.

"Humility is not humiliation, My Lady, and even the most thorough expression of remorse is not ingratiation, obsequiousness or sycophancy. You are strong and you can reform without pride, and regret without anger."

"I am sorry I offended you, James"

"You could never do that. Only by refusing to confess my sins."

As Jane got about her business I put my street clothes on and caught up with some research on my laptop computer. After a few moments I realised I was being very selfish.

I went up to Jane and asked if she would like some tea or coffee, and if the latter black or cappuccino. She wanted cappuccino. To the inevitable question I replied that the sachet contained only vegetable oil whitener: I had checked. I made some for both of us and brought her some of her favourite vanilla biscuits. Notwithstanding the prior specification, when I had bought the biscuits I had been careful to check that they were approved for vegetarians!

As I approached the desk Jane said:-

"May I make a suggestion, Master?"

"Yes, Jane, you may"

"If I write 'London' it will confuse the GPO's machines and foreign staff", Jane objected, "I better put Ilford, Essex, IG7 4GF."

In calmer reflection, Jane would have realised that the GPO had not existed for more than forty-eight years.

"Yes, I think you are right", I conceded, "Amend the address accordingly."

I returned to the couch.

As I sat there I thought *genuine Christian Domestic Discipline must look something like this.* If the offending partner (man or woman) suffers a few spanks it should be only to set him off in a chastened state of mind. The rest of his correction should involve prayer, the study of Holy Writ, reasoned discussion, and lots of warm and tender love (with or without sex). At the end he should be given a kiss of forgiveness and an invitation to the solace of the marriage bed. I think such is better than shrewing. I know such is better than divorce.

Jane was, and is, a feisty, feeling, principled and compassionate woman. She is a woman who needs to be "taken in hand" once in a while, and appreciates it. Obviously, Mary could not apply such sanction, and the Bonnard executives very rightly would lay no finger on either woman, whatever their private thoughts. The shadows of eventide lengthened as we sat, but nevertheless I hoped Jane would find another understanding husband. Jane was not a doormat or an ingénue. Jane was, and is, a feminine and kindly Quakeress: The one you always respected.

After a few minutes, Jane brought me a neatly handwritten letter in black ink on expensive writing paper. This is the text:-

Dear Mrs Michaels,

I am truly sorry for the way I have treated you and spoken to you over the time we have worked together, and especially for my late extreme rudeness, which was unforgivable, though you have been gentle and forbearant throughout, taking great pains to work with me in a constructive way.

I have been spiteful, arrogant, self-indulgent, and wicked.

Please give me, though I do not deserve such, the opportunity to prove my worth and in future to be helpful, cheerful, courteous, obedient and kind.

Please allow me to rectify my poor and shoddy work.

Yours Sincerely,
Jane Mayfield

I told Jane to put this in the envelope and to stamp and seal the missive, which she did. I told her to leave the letter for me to post and to ring the florist. She did that also, without demurral or complaint.

Then I said to Jane:-

"Whatever happens now, you have won this war, whatever its merits."

Then Jane said:-

"War has no merit"

Then I said to Jane:-

"Remove your clothes"

And Jane said:-

"Why?" with a pained expression of outrage and surprise.

I replied:-

"Jane, this is a Holy Sacrament. I have not released you from its strictures."

Jane obeyed.

I sat down on the couch in my street clothes.

Jane stood before me, as naked as a child, and as guiltless.

"Would you like another shower?" I offered. Jane shook her head.

"Would you like more pain-killers, orally or on your person."

Again a demure headshake.

"Are you driving Jane?"

"No, I came on the tube and bus."

"Fancy a stiff drink?" I offered.

"No, thank you, Jim. I am not used to alcohol."

"I think I will. Would you like a meal. I can order one in if you like. Vegan. I've checked."

"No, Jim, I better be getting back. Francis and Tony will be wondering where I am."

These were new to me. I presumed they were grown-up children but they may have been dogs for all I knew. I was even clueless about the sex of these home-mates: Was that "Francis" or "Frances"; was it "Toni" or "Tony". Women! So inexplicit!

I got up and removed a cold dry towel from the freezer, together with a phial of oil of spikenard diluted in grapeseed oil. I resumed my seat and placed the towel on my lap.

"Come here", I said to Jane, "and lie across my lap with your bottom on the towel and your tummy upwards."

Jane obeyed.

It was starting to get dark. I used the remote to switch on the indirect architraval lighting to illuminate the Risen Christ painted on the ceiling.

Jane could now see the image of her Savior, her Consolation and her Eternal Supporter. Not what I have seen in the average meeting house.

I placed my left hand gently on her head and my right on her far hip. Jane visibly fidgeted and flinched. Then I said this:-

Our Holy Savior,
    who walked from the
    Garden to Golgotha
Forgive this good woman
    her evils.
The sins confessed and those
    known to her spirit
    but not her mind
    But guide her to find
    and confess her
    further acts of wickedness
And renounce further sin.

Listen to her prayers
> **Always and make her**
> **keep them holy**
Exacting of her
> **no perpetual forfeit.**
Accept her Sacrifice of pain
> **as Imitation of Christ.**
Strengthen and Console her
In your Holy Name.
> **I commend Jane to you,**
> **My only Lord.**

Jane fell calm.

I placed some of the unction on the fingers of my right hand and draw them from her forehead to the portal of life, and then across her breasts. Then I very gently kissed her lips and said:-

"It is over. You are free to go. Go with God."

Jane seemed beyond tears. Maybe she was entranced. For some time, perhaps a full minute, she did not stir.

Then she said:-

"James, this has been the best day of my life since my husband passed away. I am sorry I have been such a trouble to you and so defiant."

I burst into uncontrollable weeping. I weep now just to think of it.

"Jane, Jane. You have been an unalloyed pleasure. It has been a privilege and an honour for an old man to hold and comfort you, and to listen to your prayers."

Some months later I happened to be in the Sainsbury's in Woodford. A unique, and a very feminine, but commanding voice shouted "Jim!" from somewhere abaft my beam. There was Jane, as jolly as a sailor, and beaming like a light at sea.

She was in the smiling society of three robust men and a fat, short woman, all of whom seemed to be busy packing her shopping.

"Hello, Jane", I shouted, "Are you still at Bonnard's?" I asked awkwardly, as I have all my life, not really knowing what to say.

"Oh, no. They closed. Didn't you read about it in the Standard? We were made redundant."

"Jim, this is my fiancé, Kevin." I shook hands with a tall, muscular man, maybe five years my junior, but visibly healthier than I. "And these are my boys Frank and Tony". Frank and Tony were lads in their late teens or early twenties, Frank bespectacled, typical undergraduates I thought. Finally Jane introduced me to a smiling Mary. Mary had lost her husband the previous month. "Mary and I have decided to start a florists' business in Chigwell, using some of our redundancy", added Jane. "Jim is the local pastor" commented Jane elidingly.

"I wish you the best of luck", I said.

The family treated me to a splendid meal. Vegan, of course.

CHAPTER EIGHT
HOLY CORRECTION IN MARRIAGE

See then that ye walk circumspectly, not as fools,
but as wise,
Redeeming the time, because
the days are evil.
Wherefore be ye not unwise,
but understanding what the will of the Lord is.
And be not drunk with wine, wherein is excess;
but be filled with the Spirit;
Speaking to yourselves in psalms and hymns and
spiritual songs,
singing and making melody in your heart to the
Lord;
Giving thanks always for all things unto God and
the Father
in the name of our Lord Jesus Christ;
Submitting yourselves one to another in the fear
of God.
(Ephesians: 5:15-21)

Marriage is a holy Sacrament. Holy Correction in marriage is the most Sacred thing you can think of for two people in their own home, except for childbirth or Sacred Union. True Correction is love, love, mutual respect, and then a third helping of love on top. Then Christ comes down and consecrates everything. God instils and conveys your love, hears your Prayers, and moderates your blows.

It must be getting tedious by now, but I say again atheists may benefit from Corrections. This is because they have souls, and also the advantage of a coherent Belief System. Their beliefs are a consequence of God's loving gift of Free Will.

Holy Correction is **not** Christian Domestic Discipline. CDD assumes that consent is given by a wife at the outset of a CDD arrangement, and cannot be revoked. CDD is a general licence for the male partner to beat the female. As a Quaker I believe that all oaths are unholy, but that an irrevocable one is especially Satanic. Sex is a Gift of God and there is little reason why spanking should not be mutually enjoyed as sex play. But the very frequency of CDD spanking betrays its essential character, and the unrighteous portrayal of sadomasochistic sex play as holiness dishonours all involved. (No: I do not make an exception for God as he is not involved).

Sacramental spanking is not CDD, and much professed CDD is merely fantasy or an excuse for sadism. Women were not put on Earth to be terrorised or humiliated.

Holy Correction can be administered to any *meantime consenting* person by any *meantime consenting* person, within or outwith marriage.

In an ideal marriage, a partner aware of his or her sin takes off his or her clothes, has a shower or bath, and presenting to their spouse explicitly requests Holy Correction. Their reason, if not already obvious, will become apparent during Confession.

Most wives and some men value rare and controlled violence as a contribution to loving marriage. Valid violence is always physically harmless but spiritually salutary. If you hit your wife on the head or the face, or bruise or break her limbs, that is domestic abuse, technically Actual or Grievous Bodily Harm in England, and rightly a custodial offence.

In "Holy Correction in Marriage" I shall discuss most things from the male perspective of a Christian man who is Head of Household, but I will presume to say a few words to female readers to the extent that I think I understand wifely issues.

You are entitled not to Correct your Wife on conscientious grounds, but if you demur for fear of the law in any land you are a coward, and you betray your voiced or implied Oath to Protect your Wife.

Your Wife does not want to be shrewish, spiteful or surly. Your Wife loves you and she wants to be agreeable, kind and cheerful. Help her.

Always remember, your Wife's Confession and possible subsequent castigation is *exclusively for your Wife's benefit*. It is not for your advantage or profit, much less for your acclaim. Neither is it to benefit or mollify any third party, except in so far as it indirectly may benefit her born or unborn children, who are her students forever.

In my opinion marriage implies consent to reasonable correction of the man by the woman or the woman by the man, whether that union is recognised by Church and State, or is an informal bond of love. But castigation should always be very sparing in all senses of the word 'sparing'. A man or woman in holy matrimony is entitled gently to enforce sufficient obedience to preserve his or her marriage. Habitual castigation, in marriage or elsewhere means that the spanker is either stupid, sadistic or cowardly. Sadists and cowards have my abiding contempt. I am myself something of a sadist but it is my responsibility to take my evil and turn it into something good, something noble, loving and constructive. Something even perhaps godly.

Spanking your Wife (or Husband) is the "nuclear option". It is invoked when other avenues have closed, and the death of the marriage is staring in your face.

If you are in an intimate relationship where you feel that legal consent must formally be sought then you are not in a relationship fit for sacramental intercourse of any kind.

Correcting your Wife

If Correction is *really* necessary, tell your Wife to strip and shower. Her *complete* nakedness is essential, and confers on her manifold benefits. Combined with the bathing it ensures that no pathogenic bacteria or fungi are on skin that will be severely impacted, there will be no drive-in, and no lasting irritation. No pathogens become air-born. It enables you to monitor her physiological condition and control hypertension and sudorification. It enables her to enjoy (yes, I mean enjoy) feelings of heightened vulnerability and submission. And perhaps it intensifies her feeling of candidacy to the scrutiny of her loved and loving Husband and the Gaze of God. It also enables her to be humble and chaste: To consider herself neither a painted whore in pantihose nor a cold Greek goddess, forever nude, forever untouchable. Importantly, it reminds you that you have to hand a living creature, the theological Image of God, that you must treat with respect, restraint and delicacy: That you must be condign but compassionate. This is not an exhaustive list.

To Correct any Penitent who is not entirely washed and naked is an insult to him or her because his nakedness betokens his good faith and his desire to resume the Innocence he has besmirched. Your Penitent of either sex deserves and requires your utmost respect whatever his crime.

Never chastise for an accident or a genuine mis-understanding. These lead to a kiss and a cuddle, the kissing away of any tears and some good old-fashioned sex by way of consolation, but only for your Wife or Husband, of course! Correction is both inappropriate and ineffective for doctrinal differences, or any theoretical construct originating outwith your household.

You never spank or clip your children. Where your Wife and yourself disagree about their upbringing, use your intelligence and assume that the mother is right unless there is strong evidence that she has erred. Your Wife can of course read, write and speak freely but not scurrilously. Never allow firearms into the house even if you are American. Discourage substance abuse, smoke outside the home if you really must, and never inebriate.

Correction *may* be appropriate for statute crime or direct offence to another creature, intended or reckless. Much depends upon antecedents and circumstances, and the presence or absence of existing contrition, including apology to the person wronged or existing practical restitutions. You cannot of course report your Wife to the Police or even her Pastor, neither can you testify against her in a court of law. You are a man, you judge, whilst always remembering that your judgement usurps God's Will and is itself a blasphemy.

Sit on the side of the marriage bed, move a pillow to where your Wife's head will rest, and settle her tummy-downward across your knees. Make sure she is comfortable and dynamically stable. Whether you are left or right handed, gently rest your hand on her far buttock and say:-

"Is there anything you would like to say, My Love?"

"I was very rude to my friend yesterday and she burst into tears and walked away. I want Jesus to take my sin and annihilate it, and I want to be a clean-mouthed and loving woman. I want my friends to forgive me."

Or whatever.

Simple, isn't it?

No excuses. No protestations. No special pleading.

"Darling, you were naughty. But don't worry. Jesus and I will help you to be the woman you want to be, and the woman you spited will love you forever."

Simple isn't it?

No long, self-indulgent lectures. No narcissism. No homilies about wifely duty and submission or any other nonsense. No readings from the Epistles.

You say:-

"Jesus Christ, my only King, we come before you today naked and glorious in the humanity you Redeemed. Please take my Beloved Wife's sins, *all her sins*, and destroy them. Please help my Darling bear her castigation with fortitude, keep my mind pure and my actions temperate and fulfilling to my Dearest Wife. Make me help her to erase the consequences of her offences. May your Highest Father help me."

Or something very similar.

Simple, isn't it?

No heavy theology. No recrimination. No bullshit.

Never lecture, preach or "mansplain". An intelligent adult knows the general character of her offence and its likely consequences and outcomes. If your Wife is *not* intelligent or is *not* of age you must never lay a finger on her.

If you are sincere and competent your Wife is already sobbing.

You now say:-

"Are you comfy My Love?"

Do not expect an answer. It is indecorous for a female to solicit violence. Consent is implied else the woman would never be near you in the first place.

Start heavy and fast with alternate blows on each buttock. Try to avoid the gluteal cleft except for the softest of pats. Aim for the fleshy gluteal folds immediately above the thighs. *Never* strike the thighs themselves: We are not here to give people sciatica. Concentrate on what you are doing and the Beloved's response. Do not be afraid to pause and break so that your Wife can gather her thoughts and have a drink of water and maybe visit the lavatory. Finish the break with a little voiced prayer. But if you are doing it right your Wife is weeping uncontrollably. Continue a little longer until you are sure that contrition is spiritually complete and obedience unconditional. Actual spanking should take no longer than thirty seconds but *do not time or count*. Remember always: This is *her* Correction, and she can take *her* time.

Some women never weep either through a natural resilience or willful defiance. The latter implies that the woman is not yet in a state of mind for sincere contrition and she must be unhanded until she is in the appropriate frame of mind, if that is ever. This is not punishment, which is unchristian and in some jurisdictions illegal. This is a religious Sacrament for the benefit of the candidate.

When she has what she needs, cease castigation. Gently turn her onto her back. Tenderly kiss your Wife with a dry chaste kiss on her lips. Then very gently kiss her portal of life and tenderly caress her clitoris with your wet tongue. Check that she is moist in case she wants or needs sex (i.e. Sacred Union) after the rite.

Both of you are likely to be tumid.

Cool your hand on a wet flannel from the refrigerator.

Make the sign of the Cross with your right hand from the crown of her head to her portal of life and from her right to her left nipple. If you contact, do so with utmost delicacy of touch.

Lead her through the Lord's Prayer. She is probably still sobbing so if she garbles a line just repeat it and give her time to respond. Never hurry. Never recriminate. Remember, love and deep respect at all times. The woman is yours, there is no urgency.

Then you say:-

"God Bless this woman, mother of my children, cleansed of sin."

The Correction is over.

Simple, isn't it?

It is time to sit her on your lap, perhaps on a cold damp towel, and to wrap her in a soft smooth duvet, kiss and cuddle her and disturb only to get her some cocoa and kiss her tears away with more cuddles as she sits on your lap. Tell her she is brave, devout, unselfish and wisely trustful, all of which is true.

If she consents to Sacred Union it will be the best sharing of the Seed you have ever enjoyed.

If she wishes to write an apology and send some flowers to the woman she wronged, or whatever Restitution seems appropriate, help her joyfully and bear the cost. Never rush or nag her.

Let her rest in bed for the remainder of the day. If she wants an analgesic rub administer one. Do not make her dress or bathe. If children need feeding or other attention, attend to them. Tell her yet again that she is courageous, devout, kind, loving, a paragon and an inspiration to all, and that you cannot express your righteous pride in your woman and you will always respect anything she says or does.

<u>Correcting your Husband</u>

As you are well aware Holy Correction is very sacred.

When I say Husband I mean your Beloved, a churched Husband, a live-in boyfriend, a male flat mate with whom you sleep or any monogamous man whose Holy Seed you accept and thus regard as your lover under God to be honoured and obeyed.

You do not owe unconditional obedience to your Husband. You obey him in all *Godly* things as they appertain to family and domestic life. You are entitled to your own religious and political beliefs and your charitable, artistic and scientific pursuits, and your separate career and finance. You are also entitled to divorce or casual separation, but if you are loving and skillful things should not go that far.

Never nag, complain, order or expostulate, and never swear or smoke!

You are entitled sacredly to Correct your Husband for any reasonable violation whilst you respect his Authority and his needs as a man.

You are entitled to refuse fellatio, cunnilingus, sodomy or anything else that diverts your Husband's Seed from your fecund place.

The problems of adultery, masturbation and the use of pornography are things many women find problematical or indeed intolerable. These things divert the Seed justly yours elsewhere to the detriment of fecundity. You may without hesitation propose Holy Correction for any of these shortcomings, especially the first.

A godly, loving Husband worth keeping will submit to your hand, and welcome your Prayer.

The purpose is never to humiliate him or take him "down a peg". It is to preserve the marriage to the benefit of your unborn and born children. You love your man and you wish him to stay:

To love, to support, and to protect. You plan to make him stronger, not weaker.

Most things I have said about the Correction of Wives apply to Husbands, *Mutatis mutandis.* Clearly, during Blessings you will kiss his testicles. Believe me, Madam, *any* man will construe this as meaning that you value his Seed and you arrogate it. If you perform that act spontaneous emission is highly likely. Show no sign of disgust and make no comment. Wipe your face and his body and continue with your rites as normal. Your nakedness is not merely hygienic. It pleases the man on your lap, and is decorous.

Never despise or belittle your Husband's tears. There is nothing unmanly about crying, especially in contrition for an offence he has committed against you, his Wife, the woman he should most honour and respect. His tears honour that woman. During his ordeal remind him he is a real man, brave, devout, humble, loving and honest. Tell him he is and shall always remain master in your marriage and your house. Tell him he needs his body and soul cleansed, and his Darling Wife will do the job. Never recriminate or lecture. Holy Correction makes all that pointless as well as destructive.

Leave him time for his prayers, and respect the fact that he may wish to pray in silence. Read him any short Prayer or Lesson he may want to hear, even if he is unable yet to believe you can Read a short, edifying paragraph or two of secular poetry or prose.

You are a good woman, performing an unwelcome but Sacred duty. Your Husband must be fully naked for Correction and your hands are naked, with rings and bangles removed. Take your Husband's crucifix chain from his neck, and let him hold it in his right hand. Do not worry about the quality of the blows you inflict: Their purpose is not to cause pain, it is to exact contrition. When the heat of Correction has died, and his needs met, a godly Husband will thank you and apologise, and really mean it this time.

A Guide for Wives

You have sworn, or implied unvoiced, that you will always love, honour and obey your Husband. If you break any of the Ten Commandments of God, or commit a Mortal Sin, or dishonour any of the four Principles of Wifely Duty then you have breached your Sacred Trust with your Husband. As an outline, the Ten Commandments are:-

1	Have No Other Gods
2	Make No Idols
3	Do Not Take God's Name in Vain
4	Keep the Sabbath Holy
5	Honour Your Father and Mother
6	Do Not Kill
7	Do Not Commit Adultery
8	Do Not Steal
9	Do Not Lie to Get Someone into Trouble
10	Do Not Be Jealous

The Mortal Sins and their contrasting Virtues are:-

Sin	Virtue
Lust	Chastity
Gluttony	Temperance
Greed	Charity

Sloth	Diligence
Wrath	Patience
Envy	Kindness
Pride	Humility

And the Principles of Wifely Duty are:-

1	Obedience
2	Respect
3	Honesty
4	Safety

A Husband might legitimately ask to Correct you for any such Breach of Wifely Duty, but it is much better if you ask to Confess your Breach, which would inevitably be sinful, and enjoy the resulting Penance.

Any good man will forgive a great deal if you turn to him with a contrite gaze and say "I am sorry, Sir". Courtesy and respect are always valued by good people.

In regard to the Duty of Obedience it has nothing to do with your external affairs in terms of politics, doctrine, interests or business.

In Ephesians 5:24 it says:-

"Therefore as the church is subject unto Christ, so let the wives be to their own husbands in every thing."

Remember that this is not Gospel Truth: It is not a determination of God or Christ. It is the counsel of Paul, a man mortal like you and I, fallible and as capable of false analogies, lazy thinking and overgeneralization as the rest of us.

The Duty of Obedience has everything to do with household organisation, children and sex.

1   **Never Refuse Sacred Union**

Sacred Union is procreative sexual intercourse when your Husband enters his penis into your vagina and inseminates you.

If there is a valid medical or physiological reason for refusing this tell your Husband what it is and insist that he seeks medical assistance for you. If you are dry, tell your Husband to extend foreplay or apply a little lubricant gel. If you are wearing a tampon or nappy tactfully explain the fact and its reason to your Husband.

(Obedience and Respect)

2   **Never Commit Adultery**

If you do, admit to it and ask for Holy Correction. Write to your illicit lover and tell him very kindly and tactfully that you wish no longer to see him because you are returning to your Vows and your Holy Husband.

Never abuse yourself. If you feel the urge tell your Husband, if necessary quite explicitly, that you require Sacred Union.

If you watch pornography, do so only with your Husband and only for its instructional value (if any). It is much better to consult pastors and their wives or husbands, or of course medical practitioners.

(Respect and Honesty)

3   **Never Abort**

As soon as sperm shares its substance with your egg a soul is created *ex nihilo*. Therefore, to kill your born or unborn child is common murder. If you are raped or otherwise unlawfully inseminated your issue is yours to love and raise without reference to the natural father. But insist that he supports yourself and the child financially. Give your progeny to your loving Husband to raise beside his children. This way you raise a betrayed and discarded child to become a loving and well-adjusted adult.

(Respect and Honesty)

4   **Always speak Respectfully to your Husband**

Never speak in anger, Never swear.

Swearing includes words like "God" and "Christ" outside of prayer; "OMG", "Bloody", and other direct blasphemy which breaks The Third Commandment. Never use "fuck", "cunt" or similar because these reference Sacred things.

Never allow yourself to "answer back" or be drawn into arguments: If such appears to be developing the magic words are "Yes, Sir", "No, Sir" and "Thank you, Sir".

(Respect)

5   **Always speak Respectfully to or about Other People**

Never insult others in or out of their presence.

Always give orders and requests firmly but politely, even to children and servants. Modern

men and women too often forget "Please" and "Thank You".
Never speak in anger.
(Respect)

6   **Always Support your Husband**
Never contradict your Husband
in public.
It is a petty treachery.
It makes him look very small and that militates against your interest. Expect instant confutation and a Correction delayed until you both have privacy.
Present children with parental unity.

7   **Always be Temperant**
Never get drunk. Never smoke. Never abuse drugs, whether illicit or prescription drugs. Always seek medical help to wean yourself off addictions and neuroses, including gambling and sexual addictions.
A little wine to celebrate a special occasion including of course the Holy Eucharist is quite all right.
Holy Correction may sometimes be helpful but is no substitute for professional assistance. Notwithstanding, your Husband is entitled to treat drunkenness or being drugged as a Breach of Trust attracting Holy Correction.
Never succumb to religious or political fanaticism.
Love without hate.
(Respect and Safety)

8   **Never Mock or Hate**
        Mockery is a Satanic inversion intended only to subvert Creation without benefit to living creatures.
        Eschew it with loathing.
        Forgive your enemies and support their efforts to be good.
        (Respect)

9   **Never break a**
        Commandment of God
        Never Lie, Cheat or Steal.
        (Obedience, Respect, Honesty and Safety)

10   **Never Bet or Gamble**
        Never seek to profit from the loss of another.
        Gambling is a Satanic amalgam of
        Pride, Gluttony and Averice.
        You cast lots for a gown of penury.
        Betting is an insult to the poor and a guarantee of monarchy.
        It will break your marriage.

If you abide by these rules you will never earn Correction and if you are offered it something will be very wrong.

Have a happy and fecund marriage loving your Husband and children, who will love you beyond death.

The key is not subjugation but humility. Keep and develop your individuality but abandon anger, selfishness and pride. Whatever your religion or none study Holy Writ for its ethical and moral guidance. But use your intelligence given to you by God. If you remain uncertain ask your Husband who loves you and will counsel to the best of his abilities.

Sacred Union, childbirth and Holy Correction are all sacred events. Delight in every minute of them, even the painful moments, and you will progressively Improve your Imitation of Christ and become the woman that God always wanted you to be.

May God guard and comfort you.

<u>A Guide for Husbands</u>

You have sworn, or implied unvoiced, that you will always love, honour and protect your Wife. If you break any of the Ten Commandments of God, or commit a Mortal Sin, or dishonour any of the four Principles of Husbandly Duty then you have breached your Sacred Trust with your Wife.

The Principles of Husbandly Duty are:-

1	Protection
2	Respect
3	Honesty
4	Safety

A Wife might legitimately ask to Correct you for any such Breach of Husbandly Duty, but it is much better if you ask to Confess your Breach, which would inevitably be sinful, and enjoy the resulting Penance.

Any good woman will forgive a great deal if you turn to her with a contrite gaze and say "I am sorry, Madam". Courtesy and respect are always valued by good people.

1   **Never Withhold Sacred Union**

Sacred Union is procreative sexual intercourse when you enter your Wife's vagina and inseminate her.

If there is a valid medical or physiological reason for refusing Sacred Union tell your Wife what it is and seek medical assistance at once. If you are dry apply a little lubricant gel. If you are wearing a nappy tactfully explain the fact and its reason to your Wife.

(Obedience and Respect)

2   **Never Commit Adultery**

If you do, admit to it and ask for Holy Correction. Write to your illicit lover and tell her very kindly and tactfully that you wish no longer to see her because you are returning to your Vows and your Holy Wife.

Never abuse yourself. If you feel the urge tell your Wife, if necessary quite explicitly, that you require Sacred Union.

If you watch pornography, do so only with your Wife and only for its instructional value (if any). It is much better to consult pastors and their wives or husbands, or of course medical practitioners.

(Respect and Honesty)

3   **Always speak Respectfully
to your Wife**

Never speak in anger, Never swear.

Swearing includes words like "God" and "Christ" outside of prayer; "OMG", "Bloody", and other direct blasphemy which breaks The Third Commandment. Never use "fuck", "cunt" or similar because these reference Sacred things.

Never allow yourself to "answer back" or be drawn into arguments: If such appears to be developing the magic words are "Yes, Madam", "No, Madam" and "Thank you, Madam".

Command calmly, gently, courteously and with manly Authority deputed to you by Another. You are master in your own house but that does not licence arrogance. Make it clear to your Wife what is an order and what a suggestion. "Strip and shower" and "Please strip and shower" are both orders to be obeyed at once, one more courteous than the other. "Would you like to strip and shower?" is a suggestion which your Wife can act upon or reject.

(Respect)

4   **Always speak Respectfully
to or about Other People**
Never insult others in or out of their presence.

Always give orders and requests firmly but politely, even to children and servants. Modern men and women too often forget "Please" and "Thank You".

Never speak in anger.

(Respect)

5   **Always be Temperant**
Never get drunk. Never smoke. Never abuse drugs, whether illicit or prescription drugs. Always seek medical help to wean yourself off

addictions and neuroses, including gambling and sexual addictions.

A little wine or beer to celebrate a special occasion including of course the Holy Eucharist is quite all right.

Holy Correction may sometimes be helpful but is no substitute for professional assistance.

Notwithstanding, your Wife is entitled to treat drunkenness or being drugged as a Breach of Trust attracting Holy Correction.

Never succumb to religious or political fanaticism.

Love without hate.

(Respect and Safety)

6   **Always Support your Wife**

Never contradict your Wife before third parties, including your Parents.

It is a petty treachery.

It makes her look very small and that militates against your interest. Expect instant confutation and a Correction delayed until you both have privacy.

Present children with parental unity.

7   **Never Mock or Hate**

Mockery is a Satanic inversion intended only to subvert Creation without benefit to living creatures.

Eschew it with loathing.

Forgive your enemies and support their efforts to be good.

8   **Never break a**
Commandment of God
Never Lie, Cheat or Steal.
(Obedience, Respect, Honesty and Safety)

9   **Never Bet or Gamble**
Never seek to profit from the loss of another.
Gambling is a Satanic amalgam of Pride, Gluttony and Averice.
You cast lots for a gown of penury.
Betting is an insult to the poor and a guarantee of monarchy.
It will break your marriage.

If you abide by these rules you will never earn Correction and if you are offered it something will be very wrong.

Have a happy and fecund marriage loving your Wife and children, who will love you beyond death.

The key is not subjugation but humility. Keep and develop your individuality but abandon selfishness and pride. Whatever your religion or none study Holy Writ for its ethical and moral guidance. But use your intelligence given to you by God. If you remain uncertain ask your Wife who loves you and will counsel to the best of her abilities.

Sacred Union, childbirth and Holy Correction are all sacred events. Always attend your Wife's childbirths and comfort her in her longed-for ordeal. Delight in every minute of these holy happenings, even the painful moments, and you will progressively Improve your Imitation of Christ and become the man that God always wanted you to be.

May God guard and comfort you.

And he saith unto them,
Whose is this image and superscription?
They say unto him, Caesar's,
Then saith he unto them,
Render therefore unto Caesar the things which
are Caesar's; and unto God the things that are
God's.
(Matthew 22: 20-21)

When you read the Holy Bible or sacred sutras or any literature including this book, exercise your mind as an adult whom God Blessed with Free Will and intellect.

Certain verses of the Bible are given more or less verbatim by Agents of God such as Moses or Jesus and you may take them fiducial. These are the verses that have survived repeated translation and re-translation in human languages. We know that they have transited from Aramaic to Greek to Latin to English or Greek to Syriac to Chinese incorruptible, and read the same in Russian, Portuguese and Japanese. They are clearly, therefore, not cultural artifacts.

After the Crucifixion and the visions of The Risen Christ the texts become increasingly unreliable. Some of the texts such as First Corinthians Thirteen were clearly written by geniuses: Sadly much of the Epistles were not. Many of the maxims of the Epistles were clearly influenced by the Roman spirit of the time with an emphasis upon servility, hierarchy and subordination. And indeed much of the Epistles, and especially Ephesians, is quoted out of context by interested parties, as you shall discover. The author of Ephesians 5:15-21 immediately went on to say something that he meant to be helpful but which has cost many men and women much suffering.

Be critical. That does not mean despise and debunk what you learn. It means think very carefully and respectfully about your Reading and your Faith, in the light of secular history and the horse sense of twenty-first century life.

For example, a man and his wife are praying together.

They are kneeling unclothed, facing each other and holding hands. Their nakedness is a token of their candour to God and their Trust in one another. They have nothing to conceal.

They take a break from praying to discuss Sacred things.

"Dearest Husband, Sir" says Wife, "It says in Ephesians 5:24:-

> ## "𝔗herefore as the church is subject unto 𝔆hrist, so let the wives be to their own husbands in every thing."

so should I obey you in everything?"

Her Husband replies:-

"I want to ask you a question. Suppose that I came to the kitchen and commanded 'Today instead of making our vegan omelette with parsley you must use henbane', how would you respond?"

"I should say 'No, Sir. Please suggest a different herb'."

"Why would you not explain that henbane is rich in hyoscine, a deadly poison?" objected Husband.

"Because, Sir, you would be embarrassed and guilty that you had made so dangerous an error, but suffer that guilt knowing that you had not sinned, but acted in ignorance so that shriving was impossible."

"Why would you simply not say 'Don't be so bloody stupid, you'll poison us all!' like many wives would?" says Husband.

"For two reasons, Darling Husband, firstly and most importantly because I would break the Third Commandment by taking the name of the Holy Virgin in vain. Secondly, the response would be most disrespectful of my Holy Husband and therefore of God his Master. I should expect and warrant the prayerful Sacrament of Holy Correction. Pride is thinking we are better than others. Pride is a sin. Pride leads to insolence and offence, which hurts. I should Confess both blasphemy and pride to the man in charge of my morals, as I care for his.

And as an observation, Sir, I am not 'many wives': I am an unique individual, your Holy Wife appointed by God to suit you, and you alone."

"Thank you, Madam, for your Ministry and your explanation. I am dreadfully sorry I asked that question, good woman. I insulted you, and I beg your pardon."

"There is no insult, lovely Husband, we must explore our faith frankly in order to continue our struggle toward the Cross", said the truly Holy Wife.

"Darling Husband, do I have your permission to ask another question before we resume prayer?"

"Of course you may, My Delight" permitted Husband.

"Is it true that muons can travel over a mile through solid rock to be detected at the bottom of a mine in Yorkshire?" asked Wife.

"I do not know, My Love, I barely know what a muon is, I am only a builder. You would have to ask a particle physicist or a geologist. But I can help you search the Internet to see if we can find relevant information. I love you so much, My Lady. You ask such penetrating questions, if you will pardon the pun."

"I pardon you everything, Sir, and you are not *just* an anything. You are a whole man and I love you."

"My Darling and very patient Holy Husband, may I ask to delay our prayer yet again?"

"Of course you may, my Holy Wife, because I know that you never delay out of cowardice but always from sacred regard for the Worship of God."

"Thank you, Sir. I wish to request Sacred Union, for though I know that we have agreed contraception meantime, and that I cannot procreate, I wish to enjoy sex that I may more closely approach the spirits of both God and His Deputy."

Husband and Wife stand and, with innocent little giggles, eagerly retire beneath the duvet. After their prayer-blessed copulation they sleep a little and then resume their worshipful positions. Wife makes no attempt to expel or remove her Husband's Holy Seed of Life, though she knows it of null biological effect, because she knows even better that it is an earnest of Husband's loving and respectful spirit.

"Thank You for your indulgence, Sir."

"No, Thank *You*, Madam, for the opportunity to express my unconditional Love for my unspeakably Holy Wife and for our mutual Creator, for Sacred Union is a voiceless Prayer beyond all corruption."

"Sir, I wish to Confess"

"Then my Treasure, we shall assume our positions" replied Husband.

Husband sits on the edge of the marriage bed and Wife lies prone across his thighs. As he comfortingly puts his right hand on Wife's bottom, Husband asks:-

"What do you need to tell me this afternoon, My Beloved Wife?"

"When we went to Holy Communion this morning and stood in the car park Mabel draw up in her new BMW and I envied her her car and answered her smiling 'Good Morning' very curtly and with a sullen, indeed surly, face."

"My Darling, jealousy is very sinful and you were right to confess promptly and without prompt. On this occasion of Correction I wish you to pray before I do."

"Yes, Sir. My Darling Saviour, My Lord Jesus, my only righteous Lord and King, I beg condign Correction of your anointed Deputy for my despicable sins of envy, anger and insolence borne of my warrantless pride in my own entitlement. I abhor my sins and I reject them with loathing. Please cleanse my soul and console the woman I have wronged. I bitterly regret the shame I have brought to the Husband who loves me despite my wickedness in traducing himself and our Holy Marriage in front of another."

"Father forgive my Good Wife these hateful sins and cleanse her Sacred spirit to restore the innocence she sullied. When next we meet Mabel, please make her wish the lady 'Good Morning' or 'Good Afternoon' with a cheerful countenance, congratulate Mabel on her new car and wish aloud that Mabel has enjoyed driving it."

"Are you comfortable, my most Esteemed Wife?"

Silence.

"Are you comfortable, my Most Esteemed and Loved Espoused?"

Silence. A long pause.

"Darling Husband, aren't you going to spank me?"

"No, Madam. I shall not. I have left the matter in the Hands of God."

Wife abruptly rose to kiss and cuddle her Husband, with tears in her eyes but no crying.

"Lie supine this instant!", admonished Husband, "And take your Sacred and intimate Blessing."

"Yes, Sir."

Is there anything deficient or ungodly in the Love these two share, or in the Respect they reciprocate?

Faith is about Freedom. Freedom was Entrusted to us by the God of Trust. Trust is a product of that father of virtues, Courage. Certainly, as Jesus Christ told us:-

the truth shall make you free.

It is our business to discover the Truth. Knowledge is Impossible to mortals, but there are higher Truths than mere fact.

Freedom cannot be enforced by your Husband or Wife, however devout and loving he or she may be.

Your Matrimonial Obedience is not about being spanked because your Husband's dinner was cold or because when you drove your Wife's car it lost an argument with a bollard. And it is certainly not about being spanked or otherwise abused on schedule in some Satanic travesty of Christian discipline.

Consider these verses of the Old Testament written by people who tried to survive in a desert, and with God's Aid succeeded:-

Thou shalt therefore obey the voice of the LORD thy God, and do his commandments and his statutes, which I command thee this day.

(Deuteronomy 27:10)

That thou mayest love the LORD thy God, and that thou mayest obey his voice, and that thou mayest cleave unto him: for he is thy life, and the length of thy

days: that thou mayest dwell in the land which the LORD sware unto thy fathers, to Abraham, to Isaac, and to Jacob, to give them.
(Deuteronomy 30:20)

Obey them that have the rule over you, and submit yourselves: for they watch for your souls, as they that must give account, that they may do it with joy, and not with grief: for that is unprofitable for you.
(Hebrews 13:7)

And it is God who is your only legitimate LORD. But God is not a landlord or a realtor and he did not promise Abraham, Isaac or Jacob or anyone else the land of Palestine or any profane thing. He promised a Kingdom of the Spirit. Occupy it.

Reader, I do not mean to insult you with politics. I mean to embrace Peace under God, and I humbly pray God to Bless you. I do not write to offend. If I have offended, please forgive me.

Never obey mindlessly: The Nazis showed us where that leads.

<u>Loving and Liking</u>

During one of the periodic infatuations of my youth a fellow student told me that there is a difference between loving and liking. He was right.

Liking is an intellectual approval and is reasoned. I like Volvo® cars: They are well-engineered, robust, long-lasting and reliable. You may like astronomy, bird-watching or vanilla ice cream.

Love is an unconditional beneficent sentiment for the spirit of its object irrespective of that objects known vices and virtues. Love is irrational, aesthetic and affective. I love my country. God knows England has defects and I love God unconditionally for he stepped in to rescue an atheist from suicide.

I like vanilla ice-cream though it would be silly to love it though I might love the female mammals who produce the cream, for they are sentient and have spirits.

My Wife and I love each other unconditionally in full knowledge of our many but distinct shortcomings.

I like Oriental women because they are stoical, cheerful, loving, obedient and industrious but though she is Oriental I do not love my wife for these reasons. Like most Orientals, Jana is very handsome, but that is not why I love her. I love her because she first loved me, stepping in to bed a lonely virgin in a big foreign city, and then loved and supported me through many subsequent difficulties.

Christ enjoined us to love our enemies.

If an enemy trusts you enough literally to place his body on your lap and his life in your hands, love him. You do not have to like him or anything he stands for. You have to hear what he wants to say without censure. Hear what (if anything) he says to God and tell him what you are saying to God on his behalf. Respect him. He is yours for a few minutes: He is God's always.

The Four Ds of Domestic Discipline

There are some who allege that the Four Ds of Domestic Discipline licence you to beat your wife: Disrespect, Dishonesty, Disobedience and Danger.

I prefer to encourage and inculcate positive virtues rather than dwell upon deficits and defects.

So I wish to write of Respect, Honesty, Obedience and Safety.

If you love your Wife or Husband and you wish these life partners further to improve you have many options other than violence, even the controlled violence of spanked Holy Correction.

But be careful not to betray their Trust with pointless, wasteful, soul-destroying penalties like standing in corners or writing lines. These are sanctions more suited to children but teach nothing, except that you are unimaginative and disrespectful.

Consider instead active apologies, repairs and reparations to whom or what has been harmed, except that if only yourself has been offended then forgive. If Reparation is under way and likely to be sustained then Correction is redundant, and prayerful, tender support of your partner is useful.

Respect

If your partner can show respect to others he or she is being respectful to him or herself and will be a long way to happiness. If your partner disrespects yourself, then tolerate or admonish promptly and gently as in "Please do not use that word, My Love."

They say that respect is earned, which may be true in some instances but I would say that respect is always merited as it is not a thing in itself (res) but an emergent characteristic of love.

If you consider that you are entitled to respect because you are Head of Household or worse because you are the Deputy of Christ then you are an immature narcissist and you are not yet worthy of holy matrimony.

Honesty

Never lie, cheat or steal. It disrespects others and exhibits your unholy pride in your own ascendancy, which is most likely illusory anyway, a phantasm created by Satan to flatter and capture you.

If you consider yourself better than your Espoused then you are unworthy of him or her and you should allow him to find a more worthy partner.

Obedience

Your Wife should obey you and you should obey her when the integrity of your marriage is at stake, because your obedience honours the God who instituted matrimony, just as I obey my Wife and she obeys me. She also Protects me, which the Church says is my office.

Never withhold or refuse Sacred Union (vaginal sexual intercourse).

Obedience is a mark of respect and you owe it to one another. Remember, your partner's opinion is at least as good as yours.

Safety

Luckily for both of us Jana has never done anything willfully dangerous or reckless to the jeopardy of our lives or limbs.

I often have.

As a teenager I daily drove or motorcycled the thirty-mile round trip to my job at Aberdeen University. During the Scottish winters I became adept at holding the road downhill on black ice and though I parted company with my bike one morning I was, as always, unscathed.

In the Christmas of 1983, fifteen years later, I left an office party at West Bromwich very drunk indeed and stepped into the driving seat of the tank-like Russian car I drove at the time. The car weighed well over a tonne but it was fitted with Michelin® tyres, designed for the dry. There was compacted snow on the urban roads and I skidded down the hill at Stone Cross but kept the carriageway.

I arrived home safely and the civil authorities were not involved.

Jana ought to have given me the hiding of my life, sanctified as Holy Correction or not.

<u>Counting and Calibration</u>

I realise that many of you are worried about:-

1 If there be a controversy between men, and they come unto judgment, that the judges may judge them; then they shall justify the righteous, and condemn the wicked.

2 And it shall be, if the wicked man be worthy to be beaten, that the judge shall cause him to lie down, and to be beaten before his face, according to his fault, by a certain number.

3 Forty stripes he may give him, and not exceed: lest, if he should exceed, and beat him above these with many stripes, then thy brother should seem vile unto thee.
(Deuteronomy 25:1-3)

This is another instance where someone tried to be helpful and sought to prevent the torturous, disabling beatings of the sort administered by British, German or Russian authorities well into the twentieth-century.

Forty strokes is well over the top for any corporal correction. The recently withdrawn Christian Domestic Discipline website recommended only 20-30 hand spanks or 3-5 rod strikes per disciplinary event and even this is more than adequate in any context.

Never use instruments because they are cowardly and cold. Favour your Penitent with your close, warm body and your soft, naked hand. Love him. Also the obvious: Instruments vary greatly in length and weight and their wielders in strength. Be consistent but err on the side of clemency.

Do not be predictable by tariff. That tempts the Penitent to count and the Confessor to do likewise. The object is to give the Penitent what he wants and needs, not more and not less. Use your skill and judgement. Take skin color, pulse, tears, supplications, struggles and everything else of the living and loved creature into account and watch for thorough contrition. If contrition fails to materialise then the Penitent is not ready and must be unhanded. If the Penitent is accepting but tears will not come, then stop spanking, shrive him anyway and offer consolation.

Remember, Holy Correction has nothing to do with corporal punishment, *any* punishment, CDD or anything else Satanic.

You do **not** calibrate the number and strength of blows to what you presume to be the quality of the sin.

Holy Correction is a happy Sacrament needed and desired by free adults who many stand up and walk away at any moment, a Sacrament graced by *sufficient* castigation, if castigation is righteously *desired*, and though castigation is likely to provoke orgasm in one or both participants, it is not masturbation.

<u>To the Woman God Found for Me</u>

I am a Christian man. I seek a woman who is brave, devout, kind, cheerful and obedient. I wish to beget our children. You may wonder that I omit to ask for Love. The reason is that a Wife who inheres the listed virtues loves perforce.

In return I promise my constant love and invariant loyalty as forever we grow and mature under the Hand of God, and propagate our kind through time as He Desired and Designed. I promise unspeakable delight and content to You, building and burgeoning, to tend and comfort You in all our days, a prefiguration of Paradise.

I am a plain man of simple faith, wholly reliant upon the Guidance of Holy Writ, which is true both in the Letter and as Metaphor, for God comprehends all and can accomplish anything. For the Word of God flies like lightning and walks with thunder, free of paradox. Accordingly I attempt, in my poor and defective way, to be Christ's Deputy before You.

Therefore our blissful Marriage will be filled with shared prayer, godly exercises and joyful pleasures, leavened by simple homely sacraments including Remembrance of our Savior, as we raise our children to be kind, strong and selfless people, not reflections of ourselves, but Images and Imitators of Christ.

You shall co-operate in our mutual Leadership of family devotions, conformable to your conscience and your custom.

I am neither a bigot nor an ideologue. I eschew doctrine. You are a free woman and remain one in Marriage. Your interests, habits, occupations, friends and outdoor observances are yours and I expect Submission only in affairs of the family, the hearth and home, and the Marriage Bed, sanctuaries under my Protection where no outrage would befall You.

Neither are the particulars of your Faith, its customs or agencies my concern, for even if you are unable yet to believe, if you marry me with good intent I shall Cherish You, knowing that your time shall come, for your soul rests in a better Trust.

Notwithstanding, you shall enjoy my resolute support along your every godly avenue, for Marriage is a unity, and I shall delight in every request You make for my advice and assistance, because a husband counsels and consoles, not dictates.

Your Mind is your Own, your Body belongs to your Husband, and your everlasting Spirit belongs to God.

But the power of the mind is weakness compared to Discipleship, as I discovered in the only possible way, through suffering.

Your wages of Your Faith and Our Marriage shall be joy.

<u>Supplication</u>

Immense power resides in your hands and your eyes. Use that power wisely, and only after calm and extended thought. If you are a religious person, pray.

If you really need something, and it must be important both to yourself and your respondent, then do this:-

Remove your shoes and the rest of your clothes, kneel on both your knees before the man or woman who holds your desire, fold your hands and look into his or her eyes and beg.

This is an ultimate gesture of respectful submission, most definitely if you wait to be asked.

No-one worthy of your love will refuse you, much less mock. For sure, he may not answer affirmatively at once, but believe me, he shall yield. He or she shall give, no matter how costly or outrageous your request. Be ready to help, but with tact and flexibility.

There is nothing base or manipulative about this, unless it is wholly selfish.

For example, you are a newly-married wife. You wish to stop your new husband carousing and whoring, and to help you save to buy a family home.

Do it.

Of course you could just divorce him, or demand that he suffers Holy Correction at your hand, or resort to any number of other remedies open to you. These are matters for you. Consider what is best for your relationship long-term.

Never nag, recriminate, blame or demand, even if you are a man of power, unless you wish to exercise your might destructively. Never raise your voice, or of course swear or shrew. Never recourse to this custom by habit, or for transient or trivial things. Only for those or that which shall persist after you are dead.

If you object that you would never marry an immoral person: Well then, stranger things have happened. It is your part to help and to salve, not to join your partner in the gutter and wrestle.

Wifely Supplication

As a married woman you naturally wish to agree with your husband. In some conventions you may have sworn to obey him, but we should not be hidebound by oaths: Oaths are themselves sinful, but obedience can be as immoral as defiance, and as dangerous. There is Mindful Obedience and there is Mindless Obedience. The Second World War as it played out in Europe and the Far East was an evil lesson in the difference between Mindful and Mindless Obedience.

Your Husband may be a Deputy of Christ, but unlike Christ your Husband is fallible. Indeed, your husband may well be immature and selfish, or merely ignorant and stupid. Before you object that you would never marry such a person, let me assure you that women often do, because women too are lustful or naive.

You will wish to exercise your mindful obedience in the service of your marriage, your home and your family in the thoughtful management of your spouse, possibly in the teeth of his selfishness or parsimony. You are of course a person of independent occupation and resources, your own woman outside the home. You can afford school fees, with sacrifice, and much else.

You are a good woman and if you are reading this an intelligent one, so you will not give way to the temptation to scream or shrew or be led into futile altercations.

If you decide to deploy knelt Supplication say nothing except a voiced prayer in a carefully non-accusative tone. Rather than say "I insist that we send our son to Christ's Hospital" say "My Holy Savior, guide us to sacrifice our pleasures to send our son to a school where he will be happy and fulfilled in the friendship of fellow scholars."

Technically, of course, you are breaking your actual or implied Oath of Obedience, and your Husband may exact Holy Correction, but a man worth keeping will apply a few soft pats to your bottom to remind you of your Wifely Duty, leavened with smiles, cuddles and prayers: Or just kisses, cuddles and compliments. A loving man of mature humility will join you on his knees to pray, to cuddle and caress.

For example, Jack and Jill have agreed a religious marriage of loving mutual discipline, firmly but kindly correcting each other's moral faults as they occur, without lectures, spite, or recrimination.

Jack has set his face against Jill's intention to send their son Abel to Christ's Hospital, a well-known English boarding school which Jack considers effete, lax and arty. Jack's preference is for Charterhouse, which in his fantasy vision of a long-gone England, promises rigorous training in and out of the OTC, braced by plenty of fagging and bullying, condoned by the masters. Both Jack and Jill it has to be admitted are victims of old-fashioned prejudices. And in addition Jack's snobberies are polluted by the vain veneration of Clarendon schools: Charterhouse is one, whereas Christ's Hospital, a perfectly good school, is not.

Jack is well aware of Jill's opinion and as they begin to argue Jill breaks off. She strips and kneels, folds her hands, prays and smiles into Jack's eyes. Jack invites Jill to assume the position, prone across his lap, *without saying she is disobedient or passing any other pejorative comment.*

Jack says: "What would you wish to say this afternoon, My Love?"

Jill says: "Darling Husband, my Holy Master, I recommend that Abel boards for five years at Christ's Hospital, because the school offers pastoral leadership, encouraging cheerful fellowship and rigorous scholarship, in preparation for a disciplined life well lived. Both this school and yours now take both sexes, and neither retain corporal punishment. But the Blues have a charitable tradition and a Christian ethos, which is not to disparage the Carthusians."

Jack says: "My Holy Savior, guide us to restore harmony in our simple married consularity, to decide wisely, and to Abel's lasting advantage."

Jill says: "My Darling Christ, wherever my Son may go, make him a man, a real man, slow to anger, ready to help, firm and cheerful, fulfilled in all his godly works."

Jack says: "Thank you, My Love. I rejoice to hold his mother, a real woman."

Jack awards eight of the very softest pats. It is no punishment or even a penance. It is almost a congratulation. If you call it a simian dominance gesture, I will not quibble, but sacramental Supplication is not about dominance, and neither about being an ape.

Jack Blesses his wife, and taking her in his arms tenderly loves her. He *does not* immediately reply to Jill's request. The Head of House must make considered judgements, in the full knowledge that to judge is to err.

Sometime later Jack says: "I shall not invite Abel to choose between Charterhouse and the Hospital, because such a decision would be arbitrary, informed of ignorance. Rather I shall ask the respective headmasters to allow Abel a seven day trial at each school to inform his selection, not that any error may be his, but that his liberty may be his, not mine or yours."

Jill responds: "Thank you, Holy Husband. If my choice of school proves mistaken, my choice of man was not."

AOT
WARREN

CHAPTER NINE
ILLUSTRATIONS

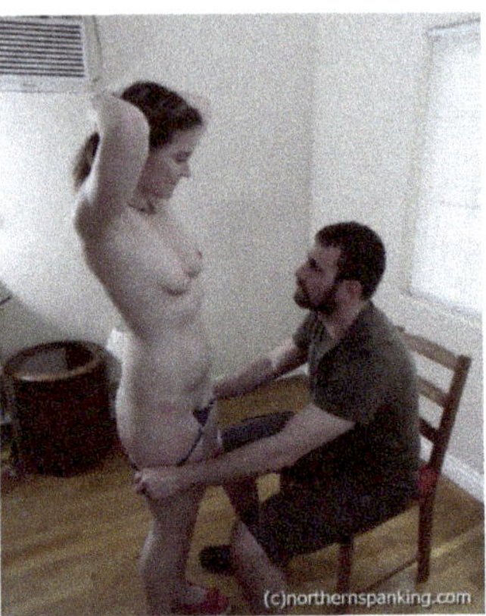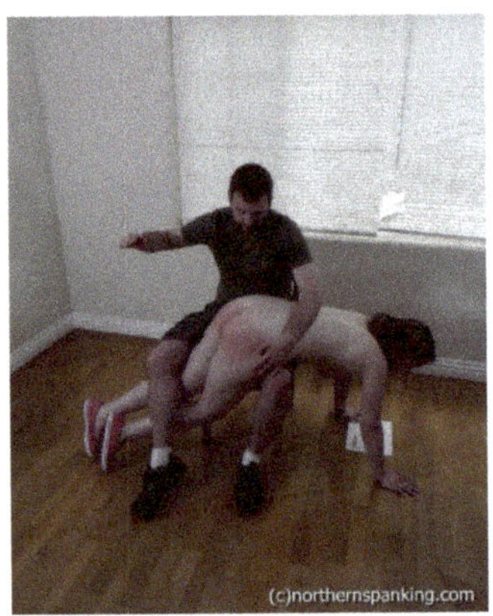

**An Orderly Retributive Spanking
demonstrated by an LDD Couple**

These four pictures are marked with the copyright of Northern Spanking, a Scottish firm of commercial pornographers. Elsewhere on the Net the same pictures are presented with the explanation that they show a named Californian LDD couple demonstrating their program for friends. I am unable decisively to establish the origin of these pictures. Northern Spanking is notable for presenting a number of amateur spankings, most of them apparent sex play.

Both participants appear to have the correct penitential attitudes, if a little solemn. Perhaps the man should make an effort to be a little less angry and stern, but he is tender and conciliatory. Presumably you will find little necessity to strip your Penitent: She is at an age to do that for herself!

The intertwining of the Confessor's legs is a good practice in this unguarded position, though it does tend to frustrate roll-clear. Notwithstanding, this confiding couple clearly know when to relent.

The subject has acquired a nice whole-body blush, and if she has positively enjoyed her experience, so be it! She will never forget it.

The major safety objection is that the subject has been allowed to continue wearing her necklace. The position is of course very awkward and in a penitential procedure the subject should rest prone upon a couch across the lap of a sitting confessor. The subject has her schedule to hand but close study seems to infer that it is a list of the spanker's complaints about her: Not at all what we want! And shoes off you two!!

How Not to Do It

The subject is in an ideal position for duration but, unforgivably, her head has been placed near a hard surface and a hard corner: She should rest her head on pillows over a mattress or soft bolster. Almost as reprehensibly the man is wearing a watch with a metal bracelet risking not only allergic reaction in the subject, but also tear injuries if she shifts. Both participants are overdressed and the legs of a subject should not be restrained in any way.

The way the subject is covered precludes both observation of clitoral tumidity, and that of the nipple. Accordingly, it is impossible to know whether there is incipient arousal, and if so whether to suspend spanking; or (with permission) to attempt her orgasm; or indeed to continue normally. Also, sweat management is partly frustrated and pathological sweating or other skin conditions rendered invisible.

Exposure of the whole body would also give early warning of some pathological pain-response developments including autoerythrocyte sensitisation (i.e. psychogenic purpura) which manifests as red blotches that do not blanch under finger pressure, and may be accompanied by fainting (syncope) and nausea. Cease strikes immediately and apply an antihistamine rub and also oral ibuprofen (400 mg) with water.

Fainting and nausea may also indicate incipient myocardial infarction (heart attack) with profuse sweating, biliousness and coughing fits. Chest or upper back pain may also be present but not invariable in a middle-aged woman. The condition is life-threatening. Cease strikes immediately, administer (400mg) of soluble aspirin in cold water and call the emergency services (ambulance) at once.

Both subjects are adequately protected against renal trauma by the position of the spanker's arms, and the position of the second, older woman on the couch enables the spanker discreetly to hold the subject's right hand and wrist at the renal position as he monitors the woman's perspiration and pulse for signs of distress. In the photograph he is neglecting to do this.

Also such hand-holding would enhance the subject's feelings of security and loving restraint, and facilitate silent and gentle reproof or warning.

On the other hand, both men are taking adequate care to avoid sacral and lower spine injuries.

The Penitent should not need to prop herself on her elbows, and her literature and a plastic cup of water should be to hand.

The (male or female) Penitent should not wear make-up. The spanker seems to be well satisfied with himself and the attitude of the spankee seems lacking in meekness or contrition!

AOT
WARREN

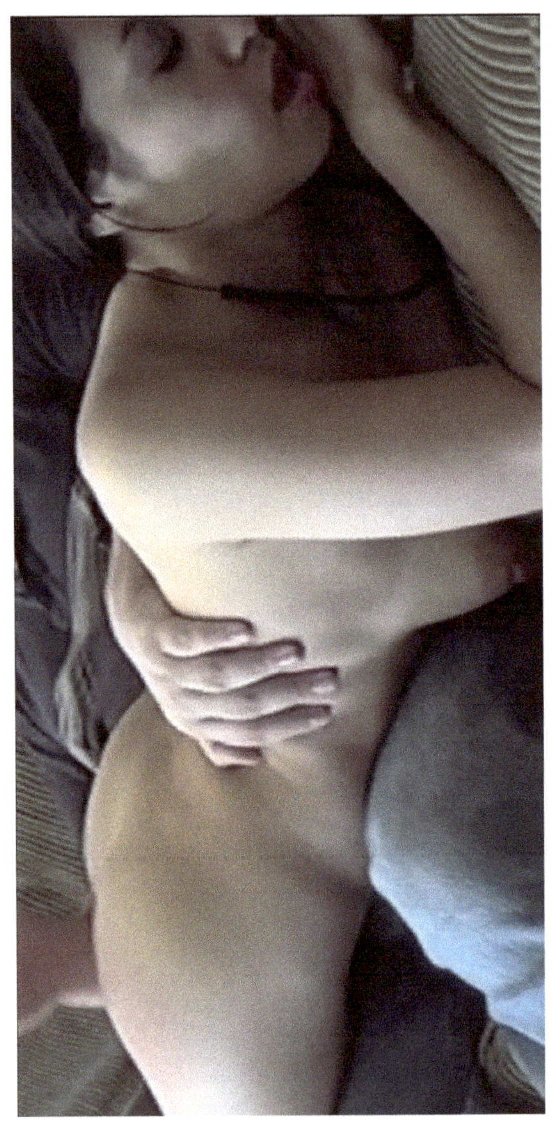

Sleepy Spankee

In the East Asian spankee position the sleepy subject is nearly naked but nothing should be about her neck. Her weight and that of the spanker's left arm should not be borne by her lower rib cage and the spanker should shift his left hand to the sacrum better to protect the lady's kidneys.

Serene Woman Prepared for Spanking

In the picture of the serene Black lady no weight should be borne by the breasts and the spanker should bring his knees together to offer improved pelvic support. The lady should not need to prop her head on her left forearm: She should enjoy the head support of stacked pillows or a soft toy. On the positive side, the subject is entirely naked. The spanker should change into soft trousers, or be wholly naked himself.

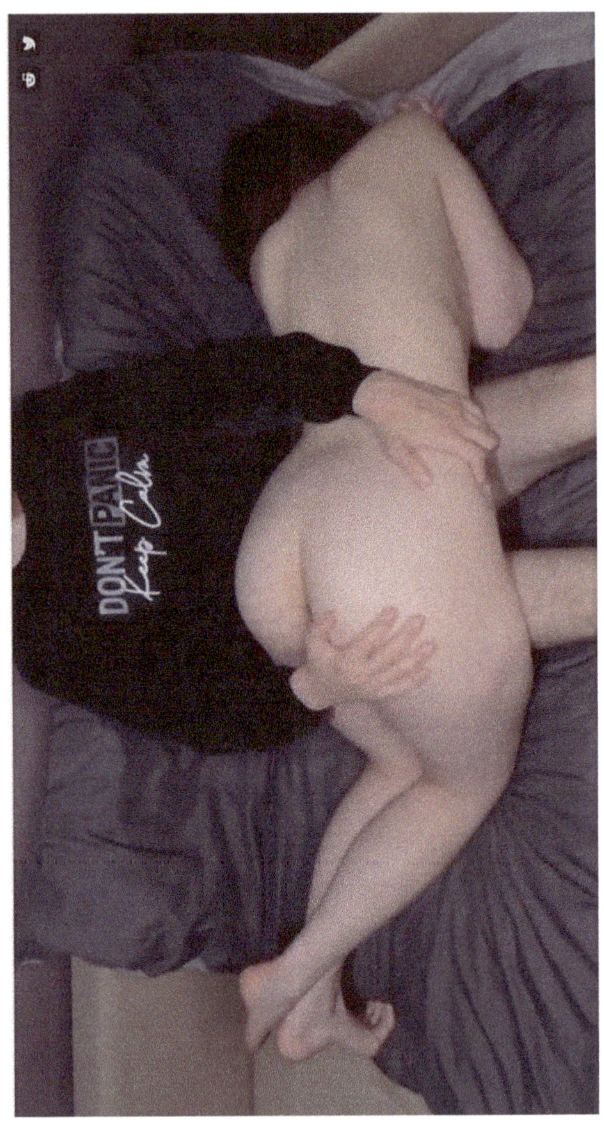

Unstable Postures

The picture of white celebrants in unstable positions is approaching optimality for a brief spanking episode. However, the male needs to support his feet on a stool so that the lady enjoys better dynamic stability supported by the man's thighs and abdomen. This will allow the spankee to de-tense, and straighten her posture. The spanker's hands are correctly positioned: His left protects the lady's kidneys and his right is correctly positioned for the start of spanking. When the hand and the bottom inflame the spanker must rest his hand on the unstruck thigh or, better, the duvet. The lady's head support is inadequate. It is good to see a thick duvet in operation, but she needs further head support from cushions, pillows or soft toys. If the spanker is naked from the waist down, then he ought to be entirely naked.

Crossing the ankles is a sign of actual or perceived mechanical instability and should not be necessary for a female subject.

Both the confessor and the confessed should avoid any scoliotic posture which may lead to serious back pain or even injury. Backs should be straight at all times.

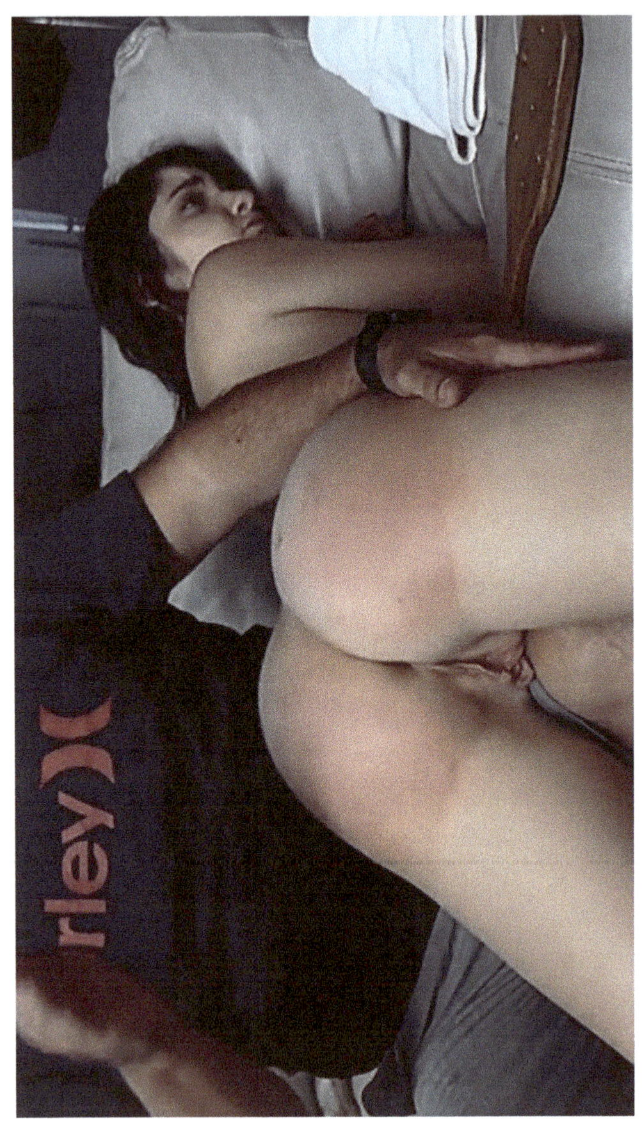

Greater Care Needed

This position is only superficially comfortable and stable for the lady but there are several errors of judgment on the part of the spanker.

Firstly, there is no place for a heavy paddle or any instrument in the castigation of anyone. I do not imply that the man might use it, but its very presence is poor psychology and no threat or suggestion of threat should spoil a penitent's experience. A genuine Penitent is a free man or woman who presents upon their own terms, under God, and they are master or mistress of the Sacrament.

On the other hand the folded dry towel is a considerate touch but should be installed below the lady's portal of life, especially as she has no other pelvic cushion, but a hard perch over the man's left knee. The wrist watch should have been removed.

This is a still from a pornographic film and whilst the lady is solemn but not distressed at this early juncture she becomes irritated later on but weeps at no point.
It is not essential for the Penitent to weep during Holy Correction because some can reach contrition without doing so. The man is not hitting hard and the film title seems to celebrate a dubious merit in long spankings.

Opened legs are often comfortable and pleasing for female spankees (and male spankers!) but should be avoided for male subjects. Slightly-parted legs can assist the static stability of the subject, especially in this inherently sub-optimal and uncomfortable position.

The Portal of Life is very sacred. The Portal of Life, sometimes known as the vulva, is the Glory of Woman and the Quest of

Man, beside which all else is mere substitution. The Portal of Life was made by God for *His* satisfaction. I say elsewhere that it is our first sight on Earth. All healthy men revel in the sight of it. To most, perhaps all, men it is more yearned for than an only son in their arms.

The Seed of Love enters through this gateway and Life issues therefrom. Love becomes Life. The Portal of Life is never obscene, or even just ugly.

Hallow it.

The feminine includes the masculine:
The text may be adjusted for sex and name

A penitent may address his prayer to God

"Adam" nominates the Confessor.
"Eve" nominates the Penitent.
These arbitrary names do not imply
the sex of the celebrant:
They are used merely to
avoid tiresome repetition of the
formula "[Insert Name Here]"

Many more, and extemporary,
prayers are likely during a
Holy Correction

<u>Prayer of Initiation (penitent)</u>

>My Holy Savior
>Guard and keep the purity of
>my confessor Adam
>Let him enjoy no profane delight
>In my pain or exposure
>Make him shrive me with
>apt words and sincere prayers
>Timely, prudent and useful
>And let him strike
>without stint and without spite
>But with completeness and compassion

Please help him God
Please help me God

<u>Prayer of Initiation (confessor)</u>

My Holy Savior
Award your daughter Eve fortitude
The courage to endure and the
strength to pray
Let her pain be light and the
chastening of her spirit complete
Take her sin and set it at naught
Restore to her the Innocency
that her trespass adulterated
Forgive her now and forever
And prompt the forgiveness
of those she wronged

Please help her God
Please help me God

Prayer for Anger (penitent)

My God and Lord of All
Please when I am reviled;
    Let me revile not again
When I suffer;
    Let me threaten not in
    thought or deed
Make me submit to he who
    judges under Your guidance
As Christ did long ago

Prayer for Anger (confessor)

My Holy Savoir, take Eve's anger and shame
Annihilate these evils unshriven and utterly
Restore to her a clear mind and a calm soul
That she may worship
You wholly and abandon all sin

Prayer for Tears (penitent)

My Holy Savior, accept my tears
as my Sacred Pledge of Contrition
Let the water wash my spirit
And relent to disclose a sunlit land
    of Holy Content
In a blameless life restored to me

<u>Prayer for Tears (confessor)</u>

My Holy Savior, comfort
your suffering daughter Eve
Let her know that through her anguish
A larger light shall dawn
       Magnified through her clear tears

<u>The Act of Contrition</u>

My Dear God, I am sorry for my sins with all my heart.
In choosing to do wrong and failing to do good,
I have sinned against You whom I should love above all
things.
I hate my sin and I reject it with loathing.
I firmly intend, with Your help, to use the pain of
penance
To sin no more, and to avoid whatever leads me to sin.
Your Son, Jesus Christ, suffered and died for us.
In His name, my God, have mercy.
Amen

The Lord's Prayer (Matthew 6:9-13) (1662 Anglican Book of
Common Prayer)

> Our Father, which art in heaven,
> hallowed be thy name;
> thy kingdom come;
> thy will be done,
> in earth as it is in heaven.
> Give us this day our daily bread.
> And forgive us our trespasses,
> as we forgive them that trespass against us.
> And lead us not into temptation;
> but deliver us from evil.
> [For thine is the kingdom,
> the power, and the glory,
> For ever and ever.
> Amen.]

Prayer of Restoration

> My Holy Savior
> Accept I beg you
> The pain of your daughter Eve as
> Reparation for her Sin
> Remove all distress from her mind and spirit
> Prepare her to amend and
> recompense her evil
> And please exact no further penalty on Earth
> Or in The Life to Come

<u>Prayer of Blessing</u>

Our Holy Savior,
who walked from the
Garden to Golgotha
Forgive this good woman her evils
The sins confessed and those
known to her spirit but
not her mind
But guide her to find and confess
her further acts of wickedness
And renounce further sin
Listen to her prayers always and
make her keep them holy
Exacting of her
no perpetual forfeit
Accept her Sacrifice of pain as
Imitation of Christ
Strengthen and Console her
In your Holy Name
I commend Eve to you,
My only Lord

<u>Prayer on Conversion (confessor)</u>

My Holy Savior, accept this life
reborn of the spirit and the Word
Teach her the
sanctity and necessity of prayer
And let her walk in
cheerful goodness always
Meek and Merciful to all
Let her doubt every apparency

Save only your
Holy Presence and Promise
Kind and loving in all she does
As you schooled us to be

The National Prayer (Cecil Spring-Rice, 1918)

I vow to thee, my country, all earthly things above,
Entire and whole and perfect, the service of my love;
The love that asks no question, the love that stands the
test,
That lays upon the altar the dearest and the best;
The love that never falters, the love that pays the price,
The love that makes undaunted the final sacrifice.

And there's another country, I've heard of long ago,
Most dear to them that love her, most great to them that
know;
We may not count her armies, we may not see her King;
Her fortress is a faithful heart, her pride is suffering;
And soul by soul and silently her shining bounds
increase,
And her ways are ways of gentleness, and all her paths
are peace.

AOT
WARREN

Manatees or sea-cows are slow and stately, beguiling, marine mammals of the warm Americas and Senegal. They are superficially similar to seals, but up to four meters in length and weigh 500 kilograms. Unlike pinnipeds and cetaceans sea-cows lack significant sub-cutaneous fat and are therefore intolerant of cold and great depths, so they inhabit the sunlit shallows of subtropical coasts, never far from fresh water.

Photo credit: David Hinkel

Florida Manatees (*Trichechus manatus*)

Sea-cows are instantly recognised by their beautiful rounded tails like, so to say, a lobe of a Lemniscate of Gerono:

Tails that they use as steerage paddles, though females sometimes use them to cuff over-eager males!

Sea-cows are members of the Trichechidae sirenian family, closely related to the strictly terrestrial Elephants (Proboscidea) and Hyraxes (Hyracoidea), the latter being the "coney", deprecated in Leviticus, but that Solomon honored in his Proverbs.

Sea-cows, elephants and hyraces are superficially very different one to the other in size, morphology and behavior but all three orders are social, intelligent and communicative.

Photo credit: Josski at Dutch Wikipedia

A Young Hyrax on Mount Kenya

The gentle sea-cows feed upon sixty types of sub-littoral vegetation and enjoy a sleepy, social, sybaritic lifestyle, in their sunny waters.

They often gather in herds to cavort, the official zoological term for what they do together. As they gather they readily use their flippers to cuddle and caress one another irrespective of sex, though should a female appear multiple males will court her and the emergent suitor bull copulate if the cow is willing. The males do not fight.

Do the manatees love one another?

Their congress seems to be without competition but blessed by an opportunity to procreate.

Ancient sailors mistook manatees for mermaids: Fabulous marine enchantresses, woman from the waist up, fish from the waist down.

There is an old euphemism in my country that to copulate is to "know" carnally.

But Woman is unknowable, as unknowable as every thing.

Should we love the manatees, and if so how best may we express that love?

Except for God, Love is the finest thing Men know. And yet, like God, no-one can describe it. The best thing we know is the Love of God: The incomprehensible acclaim we award the Unknowable.

20   Giving thanks always
       for all things unto
       God and the Father
       in the name of our
       Lord Jesus Christ;

21   Submitting yourselves
       one to another in the
       fear of God.

(Ephesians 5:20-21)

Mutual submission is the very essence of concord. We can learn from one another and all of Creation if only we are humble.

ADDENDA

<u>Cover Art: (hardback)</u>
       Prompts: James R Warren
       Realisations:
              Front Cover: FLUX (via Dezgo)
                   "A Devout Couple Consult
                   Holy Writ"
              Back Cover: FLUX (via Dezgo)
                   "Manatees in Love
                   Congratulated by
                   Circling Snappers"

<u>About the Author</u>

James R Warren was born in Cumberland, England in 1952.

Educated at Ware Secondary Modern School and the Aberdeen College of Commerce, Dr Warren is a graduate of Manchester, Strathclyde and Birmingham City universities and was for twenty years a Senior Lecturer in Information Technology and Quantitative Methods.

James Warren is a former Fellow of the Geological Society of London, and a past Member of The Institution of Water Engineers and Scientists, the Institute of Electrical and Electronic Engineers and the Association for Computing Machinery.

James lives with his wife Jana at Bloxwich, England.

AOT
WARREN